Nighthawks

John Harbour

Published by Orsorum
New York, New York
Printed in the United States of America

ISBN: 0-9710230-5-0
ISBN-13: 978-0-9710230-5-5

DEDICATION

The team within these pages is an amalgam of individuals I have been privileged to serve with and have been proud to call my friends.

It is to all of those who risk their lives time and time again, without the public's knowledge, because of something they believe, that this book is dedicated.

That others may live.

ACKNOWLEDGMENTS

Thank you to everyone who supported me on this journey, especially my wife for being my constant champion.

∞

1 INTRUSIONS

04:30 hours: 31 Jul 87

General Paul Mitchell looked at the pictures on his desk and frowned. The cobwebs in his mind were slowly being brushed away by his first cup of coffee. As he looked at the empty mug he realized that one of these days he would have to cut back, but not today. Today would be at least three cups before lunch, and probably another two after that. He was happy he didn't smoke as well, because that would only be one more thing he would have to give up in the new, improved, military. He got up to get a fresh cup and looked out of the tall office windows. He stood for a few moments and watched as the dark of the Washington night slowly peeled away and surrendered to the encroaching morning.

Across the Potomac, the red warning lights of the Washington Monument blinked rhythmically as the early risers of the nation's capital sluggishly prepared for another day. A day that for General Mitchell had started again with a phone call at 03:00 hours. For the third time this week, the satellite pictures had come back "nominal," or of no intelligence value, and he had received the bad news at home. Bad news never came at the office, thought the General, where if not welcomed was at least expected but at home where it intruded on the personal lives of those it reached.

Instead of waking his wife with his unrest, the General had decided to get another early jump on the problem, perhaps acquiring a solution before the problem itself was totally awake.

By contrast morning had come easy to the Pentagon. The General's corner office filled with an unnatural quiet as he sipped his coffee and watched the morning light slowly grow more intense, starting first with a slight hint of rose in the eastern sky and gradually increasing until the city's shadows reached like fingers, across Foggy Bottom and the Potomac, into Georgetown.

Leaving the solitude of his office window, the General returned to the photos on his desk and the trouble that they caused. Groundhog, or the President as he was known in less intimate circles, wanted hard intelligence about North Korea's new launching platforms capable of delivering small tactical nuclear weapons against South Korea—especially about their movement to a very well guarded base close to the southern border. And he wanted it now. Before the upcoming summit with the North Korean leader. He wanted hard, irrefutable proof that he could throw on the table and bring the North quickly to an agreement.

The problem was that the two KH-11 satellites that the intelligence community used were just too predictable, and the North Koreans were somehow getting the cover times of the National Reconnaissance Office's "dead" satellites. The dead satellites weren't actually non-working, but were a ruse to avert attention as they beamed the images they collected to a series of other commercial satellites which then in turn sent the images back down to an office just outside of Washington. At the moment, the possibility of a mole was secondary to General Mitchell. He had already ordered a full investigation and would let the appropriate agencies deal with the results. What did concern the General were the pictures, revealing only tarps, tents, and woodpiles. A trick that North Korea had learned well from the Soviets. What the pictures didn't contain was the hard evidence that Groundhog wanted and South Korea needed, and the CIA knew to exist.

General Mitchell rubbed his eyes with his thumb and forefinger and let out a low sigh as he leaned back in the dark leather chair to think about his options. The only way to get the photos now was through human intelligence assets. Human beings would have to get the intel from a base so secure that the CIA hadn't yet succeeded in placing any assets in or even near the facility.

Swinging around in his chair, Paul watched the morning sun illuminate the Capitol an inch at a time. A Presidential Order had given the Capitol the honor of being the highest building visible, and the Capitol in return had fulfilled its obligation to impress. General Mitchell looked at the clean ivory dome of the Capitol crowned by the allegorical figure of Freedom, and took pause. Most Americans, to the General's disappointment, had no idea who the figure on top of the dome was, let alone what it represented. Most thought that it was George Washington, Thomas Jefferson, or some other forefather. Others thought it might be the Iroquois Indian Chief. Not many knew, or cared for that matter, that it was actually a woman. A woman who represented the most precious of our forefathers' ideals. The reason for the military's existence, thought the General. Freedom. It was the base reason for everything he did. It was the force flowing as the undercurrent driving the pursuit of his country's ideals. Freedom to speak. Freedom to pursue personal interests. Freedom to even protest and despise those who protect those rights. Freedom. And freedom cost lives. It was a tab started by the forefathers in the Revolutionary War, and paid for by the men and women who had given their lives in the various conflicts since. That was why the knoll to the west that once belonged to General Robert E. Lee was more important to the General than the polished white monuments placed around the mall. Kissed by the Potomac, the Lee estate overlooked the city and all of the monuments dedicated to great men without knowing that one day itself would be the greatest monument of them all. A monument to other great men and women who perished in the service of their country.

General Mitchell imagined the perfectly lined rows of white markers and hated that his decisions could add more granite to those rows. He didn't dwell on it as it might cloud his decisions, but he always kept it close to his heart as a constant reminder of the importance and value of every serviceman's life.

Focusing again on the photographs, he started formulating a list of options to get Groundhog's intel. Because of the possible leak and the security of the base in question, he'd have to do this one "in-house" using Air Force assets and people with whom he had known and worked with before, and that presented a challenge. How? He could send the Aurora, his newest project, but that created more headaches than necessary. The SR-91 Aurora was the latest in a proud lineage to come out of the Nevada desert. A hypersonic instead of supersonic aircraft, the Aurora was more a spaceship than an airplane. The pilots were more astronaut than jet jockey. Traveling at hypersonic speeds, it was almost impossible to shoot down or even detect before it was too late and as always with significant advantages came disadvantages.

Because of the Aurora's speed and the fact that it could only land at eight bases in the world, it would definitely cross into unfriendly national airspace. In this case the flight path would take the plane deep into China who would in turn file a formal protest and squawk about the Top Secret plane, shining a very bright light in a very dark place and giving the Aurora more attention than the General wanted; risking the summit, which Groundhog definitely did not want. No, he needed something smaller, more agile, but with similar qualities. General Mitchell looked at the mahogany model on his desk. What he needed was the Raptor.

The F-22 was the fighter that would take the US Air Force into the twenty-first century. Sleek, stealthy, and fast, it was the grandchild of the F-15 Eagle with all of the improvements that older generations passed to the next. Powered by two 35,000 pound thrust Pratt & Whitney F119-P-100's, the Raptor could cruise without afterburner at Mach 1.58 and go to Mach 1.7 plus with afterburner when necessary. That, coupled with stealth capabilities matched only by the F-117A, made the Raptor a very deadly threat. Not yet in full production, the Air Force had acquired twelve of the fighters for testing, and the General had twice been to a special parcel of land in the Nevada desert to see demonstrations of improvements and capabilities.

General Mitchell looked at the clock on the office wall and took a sip of coffee as he flipped through his rolodex realizing that it would only be 02:00 hours in Nevada. The thought made him grin as he grabbed the home number of Colonel Donald Hammer and dialed.

The voice on the other end was harsh with sleep and took a few moments to come into reality. "Donald, it's General Mitchell. I need you awake, and I need you alert, do you want to call me right back or are you up?" Paul looked out the window as he imagined his old friend trying to dust the cobwebs from his own head.

"Jesus Paul, do you know what time it is?" Donald eased himself from bed. "Of course you do, you enjoy this." Donald crossed the room to try and keep the silence for his wife and daughter, who now occasionally slept between them when she had a nightmare. Both thankfully were still blissfully asleep. "Do you realize that it's my day off?"

"I'm sorry Donald, I really am, but I need you. Can you be in my office by this afternoon?" Paul smiled, knowing of course that the answer would be yes, it was one of the perks of being the Air Force Chief of Staff. Anyone could do anything you wanted them to do, even the impossible, and usually without a fuss.

"You know I can Paul, is it official or off of the books?"

"A little of both. You won't need a dress uniform if that's what you mean. I'll see you when you get here. I'll have a staff jet on the Nellis tarmac at 04:00 hours."

"Roger that, I'll pack my bag, kiss my wife, and I guess I'll see you around lunch."

General Mitchell hung up the phone and sat down at his desk as his mind started to develop the plan that he would later go over with Colonel Hammer.

The plan, in all aspects, was simple. General Mitchell had learned from studying a distant cousin's career, Billy Mitchell, that simple plans were always the best. The more complex the plan the more something could go wrong, and failure was not an option for General Mitchell.

The basis and cornerstone of the plan were the capabilities of the F-22 Raptor. If the plane could fly to North Korea, get in, get the pictures needed, get out undetected, and if the pilot would have the stamina to accomplish the mission, then the problem would turn into another "Thank you Paul, nice work" from the President. The problem was things never went as simple as planned.

Colonel Hammer had arrived while the General was at lunch, and had been escorted into his office, which he took the liberty of using it for his own comfort as he waited. General Mitchell opened his door to see his longtime friend sitting with his feet up on the polished oak desk, looking out at the afternoon sky and drinking the General's very old and very fine single malt scotch.

Paul shook his head. "You know you're the only one in this world that I would let get away with what you are doing right now."

Colonel Hammer continued looking out at the summer sky. "You let me because you know I'd just do it anyway. Besides, you're the only one in the world who could get me away from my wife and daughter on my day off." Donald looked over and smiled at his friend. "It's been a long time

Paul."

"It has." Paul took a long look at his friend. "Too long." Paul noticed the crows' feet around Don's eyes from the years of flying, the hint of silver at the temples, and the look of burning youth still in his cold blue eyes, and wondered if he had the same young look in his own eyes. The two had met and become friends in Vietnam where they had been partnered together flying F-4 Phantoms. Donald had been a green lieutenant assigned as his wingman, and Paul was a hot shot captain going for ace. Together they had managed to fly over 90 percent of Vietnam and Donald had even been shot down once bailing out over the ocean, and after being quickly rescued, had spent the next two days in relative luxury on an aircraft carrier.

After that their careers took different paths, Paul opted for the fast track of command while Donald chose the love of flying. They still managed to keep in touch and when Paul started the Advanced Tactical Fighter Program, he knew the best pilot and commander for the new unit was the man now sitting at his desk, Colonel Donald "Sledge" Hammer.

"How are Maria and Karen?"

"Fine, fine. As a matter of fact you should see Karen, she's the apple of my eye Paul, she really is. I don't remember what my life was like before her."

"I know. When Jeffrey was born I couldn't get over it. It changes you doesn't it? Gives you a whole new purpose in life, a new sense of importance. A perspective."

Sledge nodded his head and grinned, "That's for certain." Sledge relinquished the General's chair and moved to the leather couch along the wall next to the door. "So... what's so important that I won a free vacation to Washington on my day off?"

Paul poured himself a scotch and eased back in the leather chair. "North Korea."

Sledge raised his eyebrows. "Those boys gettin' a little froggy again? They want to jump at the South?"

"Not quite, but close. Close the door." Paul took a sip of scotch, "Short and simple, the North has some small nukes with their new launching platforms that they have moved to a secret base near the southern border. South Korea, of course, is feeling a little threatened. The President wants hard intel that he can throw on the table next week to make them deal. Either they have a mole in the NRO or they're using a psychic to tell them which satellites aren't really dead. I am investigating the possibility of a mole, psychics I can't do much about. Either way we can't get the pictures Groundhog wants and he's starting to look for some ass to start chewing on. Point blank Don, this base is almost as secure as Dreamland, and the CIA won't have any assets in there for quite awhile. So——"

Donald's eyes lit up. "You want the Raptor 'cause the Aurora's just too damn big and you don't know where the leak is yet."

Paul toasted his friend with the scotch glass. "Not too bad for a fighter jock. You got it. I want to use a Raptor with one of your best pilots. What I need from you is can it be done?"

"Hell yes it can be done," Sledge paused for a moment to think of the logistics. "The only problem would be outfitting the girl with some sort of camera pod assembly. I have a guy back at Groom Lake who should be able to handle that. When do you need it by?"

"Yesterday, but I'll go with anytime before the summit."

Sledge looked out the window towards the Capitol. "Has the Boss signed off on it yet?"

"Not yet, but I don't think there will be a problem. Besides, it's just recon. We're not going to be dropping any bombs." General Mitchell paused and again looked at his friend whose youthful look that was before centered in his ice blue eyes now beamed through every pore on his face. "You're not thinking of flying this mission yourself, are you Sledge?"

"The hell I'm not. You said you wanted my best pilot and without sounding egotistical, macho, or old, that's me. Besides, the less people involved the better, and I just shortened the chain by one."

The General considered the argument. He had in fact, counted on it. "All right Don. Get back to Groom Lake, come up with the logistics and a way of mounting a high resolution camera, and give me a call. I'll get authorization from the President and get you the latest intel."

Colonel Hammer got up from the couch and put down the glass of half finished scotch. "You got it Paul. I'll give you a call tomorrow afternoon." Donald shook his friend's hand. "I'd like to stay and help you finish that scotch, but I guess I have work to do. Just do me a favor and not let it go to waste."

Donald grabbed his hat and opened the door pausing before it was fully opened. "Don't worry Paul, we'll get the pictures. I'll speak with you when it's all set on my end."

"Thanks Sledge. I'll be waiting for your call."

Once the General was alone in the office, he took the half finished glass of scotch from his desk and went to a group of pictures on the far wall. There in the center, slightly yellowed around the edges and washed out from too many years in the sun, was a picture of two young fireballs, arms around each other, smiles a mile wide after returning from an extremely successful mission. General Mitchell raised his glass to the two in the photo.

"To friends and youth Sledge, to friends and youth. Godspeed and good luck."

Colonel Hammer looked at his plane "Cinderella" sitting under the U.S. flag in the middle of the hangar. Lit by the muted orange-yellow industrial lights, the dull gray skin of the Raptor glowed an unnatural mix of colors. The plane, like all of the F-22's, sat alone in its own highly secure, special hangar, each with an American flag hanging from the ceiling. Colonel Hammer looked at the camera in the corner and waved. He didn't know if anyone was watching at that particular moment or not. The security controller who operated the cameras and alarms had up to fifty to scan at anyone time, a job made less daunting by a system that went immediately to the camera that received an alarm, and since it was quiet on the base right now it would be a good bet that the controller was watching either him or the rabbits.

Colonel Hammer wondered what it was like to be tasked with the responsibility of protecting the world's most sought after projects. He sometimes watched them sitting in their GMC "Jimmys" and thought that it must be the most boring job in the world. For thirteen hours a day, they watched, and watched, and watched. He remembered a conversation he had once had with one of the SPs on a long night. The sergeant had told him that it was the only job he knew that if it was done well you were rewarded with boredom. Excruciating boredom. Sledge couldn't figure out who would want to do such a job, but was thankful that they did, and that his base had the best hand-picked security police officers in the Air Force.

As Colonel Hammer finished the thought his Crew Chief, Technical Sergeant Dave Wyler, entered the hangar and approached "Cinderella" carrying a green canvas bag of tools.

"What do we have to do with Cindy Colonel?"

Sledge walked over to his Crew Chief and ducked under the Raptor's wing. "I need to have a high resolution camera pod attached somewhere that won't affect the stealth capabilities, and I need to have it finished tonight. I was thinking of maybe here in the weapons bay, what do you think Chief?"

Colonel Hammer always knew how to pose a difficult request as a question. Usually the enlisted could put their heads together and come up with a solution so creative, it had all but escaped the higher command, and he had the best Crew Chief in the Air Force, TSgt. Dave Wyler. In fact, he was so good that the Colonel had started calling him "Wyle E., or Wyly", in reference to Wyle E. Coyote—Super Genius, of Road Runner fame. It had caught on and now sewn on the side of Wyly's tool bag was a patch that his wife had found in Las Vegas to continue the joke, "ACME Engineering."

The Tech Sergeant took a deep breath and sucked on his lower lip. "It can be done. Sure, sure it can be done." TSgt. Wyler paused looking at the weapons bay, "the problem is there hasn't been a camera designed for this bird yet." Wyly stuck his head into the weapons bay and looked around. It was only designed to carry the missiles that the F-22 would carry into battle or the two bombs it would deliver on a strike mission.

"I guess we could use the camera pod that's on the F-16. I could have one choppered up from Nellis. It might be close, but it should fit."

"How long would it take Chief?"

"Not long. It depends on how much reconfiguring I have to do to make it work. The speed of the shutter would have to be recalibrated to compensate for the speed of the Raptor. You might even have to slow down a bit to take the pictures."

Colonel Hammer smiled. He knew that "reconfiguring" was just another way of saying "how much bubble gum do you have?" He also knew that if anyone could make it work, it would be Wyle E. Coyote himself. "All right Sarge, get on it and notify me when it's finished." Sledge ducked back out from under the plane's belly and ran his hand along the wing, "I don't care where I am or what I am doing, notify me. Got it?"

"You got it Colonel. As soon as it's done, you'll get the word."

Colonel Hammer nodded and headed towards the exit. It was getting late and he still had a ton of work to do on the logistics of the flight on top of calling in a lot of favors to get the in-air refueling set up on such short notice. As he entered the warm summer night filled with stars, Sledge noticed one of the security Jimmys patrolling the perimeter and again wondered what kind of person it took to do that job without going nuts.

Colonel Hammer jumped into his own GMC and headed

across the base that was just starting, at this late hour, to shut down after a long night of flight operations. Within minutes he was entering a pin number and swiping his I.D. card through the reader as he placed his palm on the scanner to unlock his office door. Every few years the base would get a new generation of security systems and Sledge wondered how long it would be before they used retina scanners that were so popular in the movies. Probably next week, Sledge thought as he entered the office and went directly to the safe behind his desk. The intel that General Mitchell had sent was already in the safe, having been signed for by the base's most ranking intelligence officer earlier in the evening.

The satellite imaging was flawless, showing every detail— every hill, valley, river, and SAM site in the area. Everything that Sledge would need to plot a course. Not that he would actually plot and fly the course himself. No, he would be more of a high tech babysitter, an observer. He would download the CD that came along with the photos into one of the F-22's two flight computers and the terrain following navigation software would take care of the rest, creating a primary and two alternate routes to and from the objective. He would just be along for the ride, so to speak, with the ability to manually override the computer's course selection if things went wrong.

As wonderful and far as technology had traveled, there was still no substitute for the human pilot in the front seat. And that made Sledge feel slightly superior to the technological bells and whistles that were invading every aspect of his life. As fast as the computers continued to evolve, and the amount of processing power that was carried in the belly of the Raptor, they still needed him. There wasn't a computer yet made that worked as fast as the human mind when it came to adapting to the constantly changing conditions of air combat and situational awareness. Or for knowing whether the target is actually a target and not a little child playing in the street. For these reasons Sledge had to know the maps and photos as well, if not better than the computer in his plane. Sledge spread the photos out on his desk and went to the coffee maker in the corner to make a fresh pot.

Sledge was just finishing his work with the mission plans when the phone on his desk destroyed the quiet of the pre-dawn hours. Grabbing the receiver on the first ring, more to make the damn thing stop ringing than an urgency to talk to whoever was on the other end, Colonel Hammer answered a bit more harshly than normal.

"What!"

"Colonel, it's Sergeant Wyler. Sorry to bother you sir, but you said whenever we were done to notify you."

"Sorry Sarge, it's just late. I'm a little cranky."

"I know that feeling sir. I just wanted to tell you that your bird should be ready by dawn, the pod fit perfectly. With a little help of course."

Sledge laughed. "What's a little help Sarge?"

"I shouldn't really go into that sir, it's not quite in the tech regs if you understand."

ACME, Sledge thought with a sly grin, "As long as it works Wyly, as long as it works."

"Yes sir, it will work. Like I said, we should be finished around dawn."

"Fine. Get some sleep after you're done, don't hang out at the mess hall too long. I'm going to need you at 18:30 hours for a preflight."

"Yes sir. See you at 18:30."

Colonel Hammer hung up the phone and looked at his watch.

04:30 hours. Jesus Don, you really have to get some sleep soon. Sledge tossed the rest of his coffee and sent the mission plans to General Mitchell over the encrypted computer with confirmation that he was ready to go and would be in the air at 19:30 hours. The reply was almost immediate. "You're cleared for 19:30 mission, and have clearance to land at Hickam AFB, Code 31. Good luck and have a nice flight— Paul." Sledge turned off the computer and headed back into the clear desert dawn to call his wife and find his long awaited bed.

This is nothing but a simple milk run, Sledge thought as he entered the proper four number combination on the cipher lock and entered "Cinderella's" hangar. TSgt. Wyler was already working on the aircraft, preparing the F-22 for the four hour flight to Hickam AFB in Hawaii.

The mission was a simple, if not extremely long, round trip flight that would be logged as an endurance training mission. Four hours to Hickam, five more to Korea, across eight time zones and one international date line, all of that with the possibility of missiles thrown in. A hell of a way to spend a couple of days off. The only people who knew of the actual mission were the two in this hangar, General Mitchell, and the President.

Sledge started the ritual that was his preflight check. Every pilot had their own way of going over every inch of the aircraft, talking to it, listening to it, becoming a part of it—using their own superstitions to become a part of the aircraft. Sledge always started at the nose of the aircraft and worked clockwise, gently running his fingers over the special skin that helped absorb radar, feeling for any nicks, dents, or anything out of the ordinary.

Tech Sergeant Wyler watched Colonel Hammer going over his plane inch by inch. Wyler, as with most Crew Chiefs, saw the plane as his own personal possession. Something that he just lent out to the pilot when they needed it, but expected back in the same condition that it left in. Wyler liked the Colonel. Careful, cautious, and respectful, the Colonel always treated his airplanes like they were living creatures, and unlike a few other pilots really seemed to have respect for the men and women who made it possible for him to "slip the surly bounds of earth" and do the things other men only dreamt of. Wyler knew if anyone would take care of Cindy it would be the Colonel.

Colonel Hammer finished his preflight back at the nose of the aircraft and climbed into the cockpit of the Raptor. Each time Sledge climbed into the F-22's cockpit, he was struck by the difference between the Raptor and the old F-4's he flew in Vietnam. In the F-4 he had always felt safe and slightly guarded as he looked through the metal frame that held the canopy together, but in the F-22's unbroken bubble style canopy he had an almost 360 Degree view. The paradox was that sitting in the cockpit gave one the awesome feeling of being the master of their domain and everything they could see while at the same time creating the slightly strange feeling that you were sitting out there all alone, without even the plane to protect you. The other major difference was in the avionics which bordered on science fiction in the F-22. All of his important information was imparted to him through liquid crystal color displays with both manual and voice activated commands.

Everything that could be done had been done to reduce the information overload that had started reducing pilot capabilities in Vietnam and continued through the early eighties as more and more was asked of pilots who had less and less time to do that with which they were tasked. Instead of minutes, air battles now lasted only seconds. Most of the time the one who saw the other first won. But now, with the development of the advanced avionics from Wright Patterson AFB in Ohio, a pilot was given more meaningful information in less time and could activate weapons and screens with his voice to save the precious seconds that it took to translate thought energy into physical movement.

Colonel Hammer started the preflight checklist for the cockpit and inserted the magnetic tape to update the navigational computers for the current mission. One by one the systems came on line and started their own self tests, then reading as a positive green on the systems display. Sledge looked down from the Raptor and watched TSgt. Wyler finish the last of his preflight duties and gave the signal for the engine start. Sledge pushed the ignition switch and both engines came to life with a muffled roar. TSgt. Wyler disconnected the auxiliary power unit, secured the doors of the weapons bay, removed the red "remove before flight pins," and then climbed to the cockpit to strap in Colonel Hammer and arm the ACES II, zero-zero, ejection seat. The last thing accomplished before closing the cockpit was to place the aircraft's mascot, a green-haired troll, on the arm rest and to hand Colonel Hammer his helmet.

Wyler latched the canopy and climbed back down the preflight ladder, pulling it away from the aircraft as he moved to push the button that would open the hangar doors and unleash the deadly Raptor. Once the doors were fully open, TSgt. Wyler came to attention and gave the Colonel his customary salute as the F-22 lurched forward from the added throttle and began taxiing out of the hangar, beginning the mission at 19:28 hours.

Colonel Hammer looked at the flight clock and reset it to zero as he made a note on his knee board to the actual time of 19:28 hours.

"Blackjack tower, this is Whisper One. Request taxi to runway 33, departure following engine run-up, copy."

"Whisper One, that's a roger. Cleared to taxi to runway 33. Security has informed us that the area is secure, you're cleared for take off and heading according to flight plan. Wind is at five knots out of the east, barometric pressure is 30.25 and falling. Copy?"

"Copy that Blackjack tower, wind at five out of the east, barometric pressure 30.25 and falling, filing flight plan omega one."

Colonel Hammer brought the F-22 to the engine run-up area at the end of the runway and proceeded with the preflight engine check. Within seconds the engine display turned green and Sledge pushed the throttle to full military power and released the brakes. The F-22 accelerated down the runway and lifted into the evening air as Colonel Hammer settled in for the first leg of a very long flight.

The first tanker rendezvous was scheduled for 20:30 hours

— one hour from take off and, at his current speed, almost at the edge of the Raptor's range. The tanker was out of Beale AFB in California and had left at an earlier time to be in the proper location when Sledge arrived. Since this unit was the only one cleared to work with the F-22 program, they would have to have three planes take off at staggered intervals, each farther along the Raptor's flight path to be in position when the fighter needed more fuel.

Sledge checked his watch and scanned the surrounding skies. Cruising at fifty thousand feet had made them empty and open. All the other air traffic was below him and all he had to worry about were the tops of some very ominous looking thunderheads heading towards him. Sledge scanned the Raptor's displays and gave the fighter one more check before turning on the auto pilot. Now it was just him, the sky, and the plane. Sledge reached down to the helmet bag on the floor to see if he had packed a candy bar or something to snack on and found a surprise gift from his Crew Chief—a portable CD player with ten assorted disks and a note. "Please return CD player with Cindy when finished. Good Luck —Wyly." Damn it's good to have a Crew Chief like Wyly, Sledge thought as he selected one of the rock CDs and plugged the cord of the player into the auxiliary input jack of the F-22.

2 NASCENT

14:00 hours: 07 Jan 86

The Pentagon. Big. Powerful. Impressive. The heart and brains of the military, thought Colonel Mulgrave as he entered the last of the many hallways and checkpoints it had taken him to get to his final destination. He, of course, had been here before but not for the reason he was here today. Today he was here for his own destiny, his own career, his own idea.

Stopping just long enough to ensure that everything was in order and that his uniform was impeccable, Colonel Mulgrave entered the anteroom of General Mitchell's office. "Colonel Mulgrave to see General Mitchell please." The words came out crisp, confident and direct.

"The General is expecting you sir. I'll inform him that you're here." The General's adjutant, a young captain in a very starched, perfectly pressed uniform, picked up the phone and informed the General of his appointment.

"You may go right in Colonel."

Colonel Mulgrave cleared his throat, half from a nervous

cough and half in an attempt to loosen the throat muscles which out of anticipation had started to constrict. "Thank you Captain." Colonel Mulgrave paused just before the door to make certain his mind was clear and sharp and then, after taking a deep breath to steady his nerves, entered. Walking directly to the center front of the General's desk, stopping, and in the perfect form that grew out of years in the military, Colonel Mulgrave came to perfect attention.

"Sir, Colonel Mulgrave reporting as ordered."

"At ease Colonel." The General leaned back into the oversized leather chair and looked at the Colonel before him. He had learned in his many years of leadership that you could tell a lot from the way a person carried themselves, and if first impressions really did count for much, which they did, then this man was going to go very, very far. "You're the one that requested this meeting Colonel, so what can I do for you?"

"Sir, I have an idea that I would like to run by you for your approval."

"I see. And you didn't bring this up the chain of command because?"

"I think you'll understand when I tell you my idea. As much as I believe in the chain of command, the less people that know about this, the easier it will be in the long run. It's a very sensitive issue."

Nice job handling that one Colonel, thought the General. He considered offering the Colonel a seat, but instead decided to see how he handled pressure.

"Very well Colonel, what's your idea?"

"Sir. I believe that we have a problem, and I believe that I have the answer. To get right to the point, I would like to develop a team. A very special team for the Air Force. Using only the most qualified individuals that I can find. This proposed team would take over the role of pararescue for top secret programs and operations. It would be a small, self-sufficient team that would be able to travel anywhere in the world, at any time, and be able to do so covertly." Colonel Mulgrave took a deep breath before hitting his closing point which could either win his case or kill his career.

"It is my opinion that there is a large weakness in our overall ability to be able to rescue our own pilots, without using the help of the other branches of the service, especially in the category of black operations. If, for instance, we were to lose an F-117 or even the Aurora, as small of chance as that is, we at the present have no way of keeping the integrity of the original operation contained. If we had a team such as the one I propose, we could extract the pilot, ensure that there are no traces of the aircraft, and keep the entire operation secure."

The Colonel finished and waited for the General to respond. The beat of his pulse inside his head marked the time as well as the clock on the General's desk. *Well, he either agrees with me, or I've just made the largest mistake of my career.* Colonel Mulgrave tried to read the General's face and decided then and there that he would never play poker with the man seated in front of him. For fun or money.

General Mitchell sat forward in his chair. *All right Colonel, you've made it this far. Now let's see just what you're made of.* "And who, in your opinion, would be top choice to command this team?"

Even though his military bearing was perfect on the outside, Colonel Mulgave's inside was now jumping with excitement as he looked directly into the eyes of the General.

One more hurdle, and the team is mine, Colonel Mulgrave thought as he summoned forward the most confidence available and answered. "I would sir."

"I see. And what about special training Colonel? I'm sure that the team would need some. Where would you suggest that we accomplish that?"

"The training would be done piecemeal at various military schools, getting the best from the best. If one service is better at something than another we would use their school. They wouldn't go until I believed that they were as good as they could be."

General Mitchell glanced out at the cold, gray, January sky and then back at the Colonel.

"Very well then Colonel, I think your idea has some merit. Put together a package and have a courier deliver it."

"Actually sir, I already have something put together." Colonel Mulgrave reached into his briefcase and brought out a plain brown folder and placed it on the desk in front of the General.

"Very good Colonel, I'm impressed. I like to see people prepared. I'll take a look at this and make a decision. You may have just gotten yourself a team Colonel. But, and this is a big B-U-T. If I decide that there is a need for such a team, and if I decide that you're the man to lead them, they don't go until I think they're ready. Is that understood?"

"Yes sir."

"If I decide affirmative to everything that you've proposed, you'll report directly to me."

"Yes sir, thank you sir."

"Oh, and Colonel, nice move. It took balls to come here and face the tiger with a problem. Dismissed."

Colonel Mulgrave came to attention and saluted the General who returned his salute a little less crisply, did a perfect about-face and exited the office. He was half way out of the building when he finally allowed himself the luxury of a smile.

19:47 hours local: 2 Aug 87

Aside from the refueling, the flight was without incident, and Sledge started to get a feel for the boredom that the Sergeant from security had talked about. Sledge let his mind wander. With nothing to do, the mind tries to compensate by focusing on different things, obscure things, things that usually you didn't have the time to think about. But it didn't help. In the faint amber glow of the nighttime cockpit, even the CDs that Wyly had given him had become boring. Thank god for modern technology, Sledge thought as he looked at the F-22's flight computer showing only another 00:42 minutes until Hickam AFB. Cruising at eight hundred miles per hour the distance between any two points shrank considerably and Sledge wondered what it was like for the tanker crews who didn't have the speed of the Raptor. Well, at least they have someone to talk to, Sledge thought as he glanced at the night sky outside of the cockpit.

At the end of a taxi way at Hickam, a curious hangar that had been paid for by an unknown unit, locked and sealed by the same, sat untouched. Not even the base commander knew what was inside, only that the keys were in a safe in base operations, and that only he and his deputy commander had the authority to access them or know of their existence.

Earlier in the afternoon an unmarked plane with proper

clearances and codes had landed carrying a group of anonymous personnel dressed in nothing but black s.w.a.t. style camouflage. It had immediately gone to the edge of the taxi way that held the hangar, and waited. Base security had, of course, immediately responded whereupon the ranking security officer was told to open envelope Tango-five in the control center, sign the appropriate secrecy agreements, and then to forget what they had seen.

At 20:30 hours local time Hawaii, Hickam tower received a phone call on the secure line from the Pentagon, informing them that there was an inbound flight, Code 31, and to strictly follow that code's protocol. MSgt. Hiller, senior air controller on duty, went to the safe and pulled the sealed enveloped marked 31 on the cover and proceeded to read the instructions.

"Well, this looks like fun," the MSgt. said as he relocked the safe, gave the tumbler the required number of spins, and signed the access log. "Alright people listen up. We need to call the base commander and tell him we have a Code 31 inbound, and then follow the instructions within this folder. Also call Security Control and inform them that we have a Code 31 inbound. I need to make sure this is authentic."

Colonel Hammer looked at the flight computer to check the time and punched in the frequency of Hickam Tower on his radio.

"Hickam Tower, this is Whisper One. Fifteen out, I am Alpha Bravo copy, Alpha Bravo."

"Jesus, they don't give you much time." MSgt. Hiller said before heading out of the control center.

"Whisper One we copy and are ready. Notify when five out copy."

"Copy that Hickam. Notify when minus five."

Sledge turned off the auto pilot and started making the final adjustments for landing.

After the hours of not doing anything it felt good to have something to be involved in. Sledge watched the lights of Honolulu appear in the distance and wondered, briefly, what people on the base thought as power was shut off to the main electrical grid. Every essential function—hospital, air traffic control, and the runway—switched to auxiliary power as the rest of the base residents cursed as their televisions went dark along with the rest of the base.

At five minutes out, Colonel Hammer called Hickam Tower and notified them of his position. Hickam Tower had already implemented the Code 31 and had cleared all air traffic from the area, invoking unanswerable questions from other pilots as to who or what Whisper One was, and at five minutes out proceeded with the Code 31 and killed all power to the base.

Colonel Hammer had the base in sight when the blackout went into effect and saw the eerie effect of having a lit area turn into a black hole with runway lights on the edge. Making his turn from base to final, Sledge wondered what was going on in the minds of the air traffic controllers who by now would be wondering why there wasn't anything on their radar screens. Whisper One prepared for final approach and finally lowered his landing gear, simultaneously appearing on their screens as approaching the runway threshold.

The landing, even in darkness, was perfect as usual and Colonel Hammer proceeded to the unmarked hangar at the end of the taxi way. Once inside, a select crew from Groom Lake, who had arrived earlier, now refueled and checked over

"Cindy".

An office off of the hangar had been made into a makeshift bedroom by one of the earlier arrivals and Colonel Hammer glanced at his bed and had to smile. He had expected nothing more than a cot, but the Code 31 had given his team total access to the base, giving them license to "appropriate" anything that was required for the mission. A bed had been the first thing "appropriated" along with a cooler filled with ice and cold soda. A simple note was attached, "Sorry it's not scotch, but you have work to do...Good luck. Paul." Sledge smiled. About the only thing he could have wanted was a hot shower and that didn't seem very available. Oh well.

Just then one of the team from Groom Lake entered with a set of jogging clothes and keys.

"Sir. We've made arrangements to have a Jimmie parked out back. If you want, you can use these jogging clothes to go to the base gym for a shower." Sledge grabbed a Coke from the cooler and started to change into the jogging suit when the thought struck him that the advance team probably hadn't eaten since lunch and he had decided to skip dinner for a little extra sleep. "Sarge, have some pizzas delivered to the Security Police command center, and have one of our 'friends' from this afternoon pick it up. Actually get one for me, as many as the crew here wants, and a few for our 'friends' over at security." Almost as an afterthought Sledge added. "They signed secrecy agreements right?"

"Yes sir."

"Good." Sledge knew that it was taking a risk getting the pizza, but this wasn't war he told himself, and no one would be looking here until it was too late. Nothing he did would disrupt mission integrity. Much. "Oh, and Sarge, remember to make mine double cheese."

"You got it Colonel."

The shower was warm and Sledge closed his eyes and thought about his wife and daughter. Maria had understood that he would be gone for a few days on a temporary assignment. And she understood that her husband did important things for their country in the desert. She just didn't have to like it.

Sledge thought about sending some flowers. She'd put up with his lifestyle for long enough. Roses. Lots and lots of roses, Sledge thought but then realized that ordering flowers would be just a little too much to explain on the expense account and he couldn't very well call from Hawaii with his credit card could he? Oh fuck it. Sledge quickly got dressed and found the nearest pay phone to the locker room. He would have the call transferred through Wyly back at Groom Lake so that it wouldn't show up on his phone bill as a call from the aloha state.

After calling in the flower order, Sledge jumped into his Jimmy and drove the five minutes back to the hangar, the last two with his lights off, to find that the Security Police Sergeant from earlier had already delivered the pizzas and Sledge's double cheese was waiting for him as the rest of the team was in the process of getting rid of their own "evidence." Thirty minutes. Not too bad, Sledge thought as he grabbed a slice and plopped down in the leather couch someone from his unit had "appropriated" from the Base Exchange. The couch had been paid in full, of course, in cash, and was to be donated to the recreation center when they left.

Leaving Hickam at 00:00 hours timed the remainder of the flight so that Colonel Hammer would arrive over North Korea at approximately 02:00 hours their time, yesterday. Hopefully the crews at the SAM sites, like most of those around the world who worked nights, would have just finished eating their "lunch" and would not be quite as alert as usual due to the blood rushing to their digestive systems, adding another, if slight, advantage to the Raptor.

The power again had been shut off as Whisper One taxied to the runway without so much as a hint of stopping for an engine run-up. The minor annoyance that had occurred earlier as a surprise again returned and cloaked the base in darkness until Colonel Hammer was clear of the area by a full five minutes. Once again Sledge applied full military power and the Raptor streaked down the runway and eased into the air. Sledge watched as the lights of the runway slid away behind him into the darkness like cobalt blue fireflies and the F-22 disappeared into the tranquil Hawaiian night. Sledge checked the navigational screen and double checked that the coordinates of his next waypoint were correct and settled back for another long ride into the night sky. Since this flight would be the actual mission, it would be more than twice as long as the flight to Hickam, almost a full ten hours and Colonel Hammer was thankful for the extra sleep he had allowed himself at Groom Lake.

Three CDs and nearly eleven hundred miles later, Sledge could see the strobe on the refueling boom as the KC-135 Crew Chief began guiding the fueling probe into the top of the Raptor's fuselage. Sledge glanced at the mission clock and verified that he was right on time and watched as the fuel gauges started climbing towards the top of their bars. When they were at their max, Sledge clicked on the interior cockpit light and in the amber glow waved farewell to the crew aboard the tanker. Alone again, and tired of music, Sledge turned on the auto pilot and tried to determine his position by the stars. His mind flashed thoughts of his wife and daughter and Sledge pulled out the maps to go over the mission one last time.

In the distance, the lights from Tokyo began filling the night sky with the usual glow of a city. Sledge checked the computer and made the calculations required for his last refuel to top off his tanks before going into Korea. Like before he watched, almost hypnotized, as the probe from the KC-135 approached the front of his aircraft and slowly slid into place and locked. After the refueling was complete, Sledge again waved to the tanker crew and realized that this would be the last friendly aircraft he would see for a while.

Five minutes out of North Korea, Sledge finished a protein bar for energy and checked the weapons computer to make sure the air-to-air missiles were on-line and armed. Just in case, Sledge thought, just in case.

3 RESCUE TEAM ALPHA

08:30 hours: 17 Jun 86

It was only mid-morning and already the temperature was soaring into the 90's as the sun cut through the dry crystal blue sky. Sgt. Chris Ross turned right off of Las Vegas Boulevard on to the main entrance road of Nellis Air Force Base, and pulled up to the main gate. The gate house was standard USAF except for the fact that it, as everything else on the base, was not painted Air Force blue but the color of desert tan. Chris rolled down his window as the Security Police officer approached his car.

"Morning Airman. Could you tell me how I would get to building 812?" Sgt. Ross asked as his ID was checked. A slight smile came over the Airman's face. "Sarge, that building doesn't exist."

"Well, I have an appointment there in twenty minutes. Could you check the base directory for me please."

The Airman's face became serious. "It's a joke Sarge. The building isn't supposed to exist if you know what I mean." The Airman smiled, "Just go to the main road past the BX and take a left. Follow that road all the way to the end of the base, just about when you think you're lost, you'll see the building."

"BX and take a left, fall off the face of the earth. Got it, thanks."

"Oh and Sergeant, be careful. People go into that building, but I never see them come out again," again the Airman smiled, a big toothy smile, and waved Sgt. Ross's car through the gate.

Nellis Air Force Base was a huge, sprawling complex located just outside of Las Vegas. The base had two long, five thousand foot runways and they were in the process of building a third which was why, at times, this was the busiest airport in the world. During Red Flag, when units were arriving or departing, planes would land with less than thirty seconds between them and there was always some sort of activity in the air. Other than Red Flag, the base was also home to the 37th Fighter Group and the Red Eagles, the Air Force's "Soviet" squadron, which caused Chris to do a double take as he saw a Soviet marked F-5 painted in the camouflaged pattern of the Warsaw Pact fly by.

It had only been four months since Chris had met the man that would change his life forever. And now, due to that meeting, this morning he had stood on the porch of his new apartment, surrounded by the yet unopened boxes that contained his life, staring at the Las Vegas skyline. In the distance Mount Charleston towered above the surrounding desert mountains that framed the city which was split into two areas visible to Chris. In one area he could see the southwestern styled houses so calm and quiet as people began their morning activities like any other suburban town, and in the other he could see the still beckoning neon lights of the casinos, inviting you in for a chance to win your fortune, or more likely, lose it. Las Vegas Nevada, Sin City, Lost Wages, the town with the bars that never close, and yet in the early morning light it all seemed so peaceful, so clean—yet Chris knew that all the names had reasons behind them. Chris wondered why the man he had respected so quickly, enough to take a gamble on the rest of his career, would choose a place like Las Vegas for this assignment.

Sergeant Chris Ross and his team were providing security cover for some maintenance work being done on one of the 150 Minuteman Missiles buried deep beneath the South Dakota farmland when an Air Force Jimmy pulled up to their peacekeeper fighting vehicle. Chris and the rest of his team had thought that the Colonel inside must be conducting surprise inspections and quickly got their gear in order as Chris left the vehicle to properly greet the Colonel and possibly give his team extra time to get sharp. It had turned out to be nothing of the sort, and Chris was surprised to find that the Colonel was there to see him and make an offer that Chris immediately knew his heart wouldn't let him refuse. The offer was nothing more than a new assignment in Las Vegas. A position that required a Top Secret SBI clearance. Those two magic words, Top Secret, held all sorts of adventure and possibility. A welcome change from his current assignment.

The boredom of being stationed in South Dakota had almost, but not quite, driven him crazy. The weather was nice in the summer, but the winters were long and brutal with wind-chill temperatures of thirty degrees below zero, and a wind that blew the falling snow sideways across the prairie at reckless speeds. Nothing like the winters he was used to growing up in Maryland. The only way out of South Dakota, other than accepting this assignment, was to go to South Korea where the weather was the same if not worse. A place as cold as South Dakota with a language he didn't understand.

Besides, the man in front of Chris intrigued him. There was something about him, something pure, something honest, something real. He dealt with Chris as an equal although they both knew who was the boss and he could tell immediately that he liked the Colonel and in turn would like whatever he was associated with. He also liked the thought of a new adventure. He had always been one prone to new adventures. It was partly the adventure that had made him join the Air Force to begin with. He couldn't stand the thought of pumping gas in his hometown for the time of his youth. The romantic call of adventure rang in his ears and he had to follow. That voice was again calling his name and it only took a moment to decide what to do.

Being raised never to do anything half way, Chris had graduated top of his class in Basic Training and received honor graduate awards in three of the four military schools he attended. He had gained rank fast, or as fast as you could in the Air Force and all it had brought him was a nice little ribbon, some plaques on the wall, and assignment in South Dakota. Maybe this will be the start of my real career, Chris thought, something special, something unique and a million miles away from pumping gas back home. Something more exciting than standing on a missile silo in the middle of a thousand square miles of prairie watching the tumbleweeds blow by.

His orders had come through in just over two weeks from

the time of that first meeting, unusually fast for the military, but the only thing that they revealed was that he was being reassigned to a group of cryptic numbers, NJOTB7S7, wherever and whatever the hell that was, and to report to Nellis Air Force Base at 09:00 hours on today's date.

Chris pulled his car into the parking lot at the side of building 812 and turned off the engine. Sitting for a moment in the sunshine, twenty-two year old Air Force Sergeant Chris Ross looked at the building that would be his portal into a new reality. A reality of excitement and intrigue. It had to be, he thought, or it wouldn't be Top Secret, right?

The building on the end of Nellis AFB seemed lonely. It sat by itself at the edge of the tarmac with no signs that usually adorned the Air Force's buildings, just a number. Nothing to show its mission or purpose, just 812 in white letters on a sand brown colored plaque, not even the landscaped Joshua trees that adorned the other buildings. The security inside, however, provided a different story. This was the doorway, so to speak, to a very special piece of land in the Nevada desert, and to get there, you first had to pass through here.

Sgt. Chris Ross opened the door and entered the first of three anterooms, where his I.D. was checked, his purpose verified, and his presence acknowledged with the somewhat jarring announcement over the P.A. system of "unauthorized personnel in the building."

His escort came out to meet him and ushered him through the hallways into a room with four captains, five other sergeants, and two staff sergeants seated at a long wooden table. The walls were stark white without any windows and as the door closed behind him, the metal clack of the lock was heard. Sgt. Ross took the only seat left at the table and nodded to the rest of the men.

A second door to the room was opened and Colonel Russell Mulgrave entered without a word. His six foot-three, 225 pound frame demanded attention with an equal amount of respect. He walked directly to the podium at the end of the table and smiled.

"Welcome gentleman, I know you are all anxious to find out why you are here, so let me start by introducing myself. I am Colonel Mulgrave, Colonel Russell Mulgrave." The Colonel paused, and gave each of the men in the room a look, "and you gentleman, are a very special group of men. You have all been hand selected because of your record, my evaluation, and the special talents that each of you possess. With the exception of the pilots, some of you come from the pararescue career field, and some from security police EST teams. I have done this for a variety of reasons, however, the main one being that the PJ's are more advanced in rescue operations, while the EST members are more adept at small unit and hostage rescue tactics. I should hope that together you will comprise the best of both worlds. I know that each of you think highly of your respective career fields but from now on you will be the most elite group of the Air Force. So elite, you won't exist. You will, upon your agreement, because membership in this group must be voluntary, belong to a very special group called Rescue Team Alpha, and for those of you who choose to stay, you and I are it. If anyone here does not want to continue, please leave now, so that we may begin the classified portion of this briefing." The Colonel waited for a moment, and watched as each member silently remained seated around the table.

"Okay gentlemen, welcome to Rescue Team Alpha. The rest of this briefing is classified.

"Our primary mission will be to provide support for classified projects operating out of the Nellis test ranges, should they require our assistance. However, you will be receiving special training and due to the "black" nature of our unit, it is foreseeable that when we are finally active we could be used in other classified operations where our special talents would be an asset. You will be trained by the best and will be the best at what you do. You will have no equals.

"As for living arrangements, I hope that you are finding everything that you need in Las Vegas. As for now just know that this will be the last time that you will fly out of Nellis. When we get to Home Base you'll all be briefed on how to get to work and the other things that you'll need to be aware of. So gentleman, if you will be so kind as to board the airplane on the ramp, we'll take you up to Home Base where we'll begin settling in, and see how we can put this show on the road. Again, gentlemen, welcome to Team Alpha and congratulations."

With that Colonel Mulgrave opened the door he had entered earlier and led the newly formed rescue team to the red and white 737 parked outside in the blistering Nevada sun. Chris and the rest of the men boarded the plane on the ramp with a strange mixture of curiosity, anxiety, and excitement in the pit of their stomachs. Their faces reminded Chris of boys going on a roller coaster for the first time, not quite knowing what they have gotten themselves into, but eager for the experience.

4 AREA 51, HOME BASE

In the middle of the nuclear test range of the Nevada desert sat the most secure piece of real estate in the world, Groom Lake. Flanked by mountains on three sides and surrounded with the most technologically advanced security systems, there wasn't a thing that moved, living or mechanical, that was not detected. Sensors that measured the amount of ammonia in human perspiration provided the first line of many in a defense system that stretched miles into the desert, constantly searching for those that did not belong.

The security of each sector was increasingly heightened from the outside perimeter to the main gate respectively, ranging from observation and surveillance on the outer perimeters all the way to shoot on site in the inner ones. It was the only domestic base where the rules of engagement had been taken to such extremes. The belief being that if you had defeated all of the classified systems to arrive at the base's outer fence without being detected, then you definitely knew what you were doing and you were not there to take a tour; you were there to accomplish other, more deliberate, sinister acts. The airspace around the test site was closed to all air traffic, including military, for twenty miles. The base wasn't even available to aircraft declaring an in-flight emergency. They were instructed to land at Tonopah where security would asses the emergency and take appropriate action. And so, the security personnel at Area 51 were hand picked, highly skilled Security Policemen whose only job was to protect what went on inside the Top Secret test facility without fail. And they did.

Hot, sandy, and isolated, Groom Lake had at one time or another been the home to the U-2, SR-71, F-117A, and a host of other Top Secret projects, earning it the befitting moniker of Dreamland. Most of the Air Force's secret technology was tested here, along with a few CIA, Army, and Navy projects, each oblivious to the other projects happening around them. Each was accustomed to keeping out of business that didn't concern them directly.

For that reason alone, the base was perfect for training in secrecy. The only eyes to avoid were the twice daily fly overs by Russian satellites, and the occasional curiosity seekers on a local mountain top in the Papoose Mountain Range that was still in publicly accessible. The former were scheduled and easy to avoid. The later fueled by hype TV shows insisting on aliens being kept at the base were a little more pesky, and occasionally a security team would have to be sent out with a representative from the Nevada State Police to see if there was any unauthorized filming taking place, and to ask the onlookers to please leave the area. Usually they would comply, but occasionally a training operation would be postponed until night when visibility would be nearly impossible.

The specially chartered jet landed right behind a MIG-19 that was used in Red Flag exercises and the twelve members of Rescue Team Alpha were taken directly to Dreamland's Security Headquarters where they were issued special I.D.'s, told where they were and where they were not allowed to go, and to have their palm read by the electronic scanner that would register the hills and valleys of their palm and convert the data into a digital equivalent of a very large finger print.

After being briefed by the security coordinator for the base, the new arrivals were driven over to their headquarters, an isolated hangar at the far end of the base. They were dropped from the bus in front of the hangar, away from the flight operations and other projects that they didn't need to see when Colonel Mulgrave opened the door and gestured inside "Gentlemen if you'll please..."

Inside, the hangar was subdivided into six sections: a hangar area for a white Gulfstream IV bearing civilian markings, a vehicle bay holding two HUMVs and two black Jimmys, a supply section, an armory, a communications and command center, and an office area. Chris noticed everything was top quality, latest edition equipment. Nothing had been used. The flat black paint on the GMCs even looked like it was still a little wet and Chris looked at the white Gulfstream and wondered to himself what exactly he had gotten himself into.

The hangar even had its own self-contained security system, separate from the rest of the base. This had been a stipulation that had ruffled some feathers over at the "cop shop" and had caused Colonel Mulgrave to meet with the Security Commander and explain that it had to do with Operation Security and not the quality of security at the base.

The Colonel walked to the front of the group and quiet fell over the newly formed team. "Gentleman, welcome to Home Base. Let me start by saying a little bit about the hangar you are now standing in. This will be our operations center while we are here at Groom Lake. As you can see, I have done a little advance work while I was waiting for your security clearances to come through the DOD. By the way, each of you now has a Top Secret, SBI, Special Access Required security clearance. You will be briefed only on things you need to know, when you need to know them. I know you have all been in the game long enough to know how to keep your noses out of other people's business." Colonel Mulgrave began to walk to the supply portion of the hangar. "In fact, that's one of the qualifications for being chosen. Now, if you gentleman will follow me, I'll give a quick tour before we begin our official briefing.

"This is the supply section of the hangar. Since we are a small unit, and intend to keep it that way, we don't have a supply detachment. We will take care of ourselves. Sgt. Hoffman will be in charge of supply and will let me know what I need to 'acquire' from other units." As he said acquire a small smile came over the Colonel's face. Finally, Chris thought, a commander who knows how to get things done.

"As you may have noticed earlier, a lot of the people on this base wear civilian clothes and non-regulation hair cuts. You might have assumed that they were civilian contractors. They're not. Most of them are military. Their projects dictate what to wear. For us, however, I am sorry to say, that won't be the case so don't get your hopes up. Because of the nature of our mission, I still want a military image. So for everyone except the pilots appearance regulations are still in effect. The four pilots, for operational reasons only, will be able to wear their hair a little longer. I still want to have the utmost in professionalism and military bearing, so that brings us to uniforms. While you are here on site you will wear what you need for the job. Example, if we have a training exercise in the desert, you will wear desert camouflage. However, if you have been assigned to duties here in the hangar, communications for example, you may wear civilian clothes. Okay? Good. The only thing different is that your uniforms will no longer have any official markings. You will be issued nine sets of new uniforms: three sets of desert, three sets of woodland, and three sets of black BDU's. They will not, I repeat, will not have any markings. With what we are going to be doing, you don't need them. Any questions yet?"

Colonel Mulgrave looked at the faces of each of the men in the room. Perfect. Not one of them blinked at the thought of what they might be called to do. Each held his gaze firmly, confirming assessments he'd made long ago. "Good, let's move on. This next section is the communications area. This is the best equipment I could find. With it we can uplink to our satellites and communicate securely anywhere in the world," again a sly smile came across Colonel Mulgrave's face. "And if the NSA calls, we don't have it."

The rest of the tour was just as intriguing. There were two Jimmys painted flat black, two Hummers parked next to them painted the same; a white Gulfstream with civilian markings that looked like it came right off the assembly line, until you looked inside and saw all of the advanced avionics and modifications made to the interior so that the door could be opened in flight; and an armory with the best weapons money could buy from Glock 9mm, M-16's, and 9mm H&K's MP-5 assault rifles. It was like a candy store for a quick response team. Anything and everything a team could want was at their disposal: radios, night observation devices, and all the other tools necessary for their purpose. Nothing had been forgotten. It was then that Chris realized that Colonel Mulgrave was not one to leave anything to chance. He gave his men the best equipment and training and in return for that if he ordered something done, he wanted, expected, and accepted nothing less than perfection in the execution of those orders.

Chris looked at the other members of the team. All were in excellent shape, and their uniforms were in perfect order. Each member looked like they had stepped out of a recruiting poster. All of the eyes were clear and sharp, the kind of eyes where you can see right through to the intelligence behind them. The kind that scared you in an enemy but found comforting in a friend. The kind you knew that if you happened to be foolish or intoxicated enough to get into a fight, they would be one step behind you without a second thought. Loyalty. You could see it in their eyes. I would definitely trust my life with these guys. He wondered if they were thinking the same.

Each member had been hand picked very carefully by Colonel Mulgrave. He had asked the records department at Randolph AFB in Texas to locate fifty people who had been honor graduates in at least two of their military schools, received good conduct medals or any awards for merit, had exemplary performance reports, and outstanding records. The only other stipulation was that ten be pilots, captain and above, and that the rest be NCO's half from the Pararescue career field, half from the Security Police career field preferably from Emergency Services Teams, and all be under thirty.

From those fifty he had selected twenty-five who he sent, with a little help from the Pentagon, agents from the Air Force Office of Special Investigations. The AFOSI agents then worked undercover with each, developing friendships and bonds with them, digging deeper and deeper to see who they really were.

After each report had been carefully screened by the Colonel, he then proceeded with background checks on fifteen of them. After those had come back and he was reasonably sure that their clearances would be no problem he approached the top twelve personally, offering each an assignment that he couldn't tell them about. He had expected one or two to decline and then he would move farther down to the others on his list, but to his surprise he didn't have to. Now they were all assembled in this hangar, and Chris looked at all of them not realizing the process that he and all of them had been through. They were the best, although none of them knew it, and after the Colonel was through with them they would be even better.

Colonel Mulgrave cleared his throat and began the briefing. "Gentleman, I am going to make this briefing as informal and short as possible. I hope what you have seen so far indicates to you how serious I am about the success of this team, and the safety of all of you. I've tried to give you all of the best out there, and beginning next week you will all be receiving highly advanced, specialized training. We'll go more into that later, but first the ground rules. Unless it's an emergency, to get to work you will now go to the Hughes Hangar at McCarran International Airport. From there you will be able to catch the Department of Energy's red and white 737 up to here. Schedules are in the packets that I'll give you at the end of today. These are not classified, but they are sensitive so be careful with them.

"Your schedule for work, when you are not training, will be four days on and four days off. You, of course, can use all the facilities at Nellis, especially things like medical and dental, but try to limit your exposure on the base. Don't hang out at the NCO and Officers' clubs, or get too involved with the base. Although we can use Nellis, we aren't officially stationed there and we don't want to cause too much curiosity.

"Now as for here at work, you will be broken into two teams of six each consisting of: two pilots, a team leader, assistant team leader, and two members, in other words, a basic fire team with two pilots. Each team will rotate with the other every four days, and while you are here at Groom Lake you will be on call twenty-four hours a day. You will have various duties during the day, and the nights belong to you, just keep a radio or beeper with you so the control center can get in touch with you. Speaking of free time, there is a gym, club, and small library at what the Air Force wants to call a recreation center, and if you want, there's a pool over at the Tonopah Test Range that you can use if you want to make the drive.

"As for your working hours, each of you will rotate through certain jobs, like the communications center, and since we still are an Air Force unit, there will still be paperwork and reports to fill out. Like I said before, when you are working here in the hangar you may wear civilian clothes. And that leads me to the other point I want to clarify." Colonel Mulgrave gestured to the white Gulfstream. "As you may have noticed, the Gulfstream has civilian markings. In keeping with that cover, the pilots of the team will be wearing corporate attire when they fly outside of the test range. You may still wear flight suits when you are flying "on range," and you may now also grow your hair a bit longer to look more like a civilian, but remember that you are corporate pilots, and should still be clean cut. You now fly, not for the Air Force, but for NDB Energy. Okay. Good."

Colonel Mulgrave walked over to a desk and pulled out information packets and handed one to each of the team members. "Here are your packets gentleman. Inside is everything that you need to know that I haven't yet covered. The NCO's will find information in theirs about the training they will start. The pilots will find information on the course you are going to be taking from our friends over at skunk works on the modifications they have made to the Gulfstream and how it will effect the flight characteristics. There is also some information on local housing in Vegas for those of you who haven't found anything permanent yet.

Okay gentleman, the rest of the day is yours. Use it to get acquainted with the base and each other before you catch the freedom bird back to Las Vegas. Catch the early flight tomorrow, and report back here at 0900. Dismissed." With that the team went to familiarize themselves with the new base and boarded the group's own brand new blue goose, Air Force bus, and drove to the living area.

The living conditions on the base were far from extravagant, to say the least. Since the base had been born in secrecy, the Air Force had opted not to build large barracks and instead had brought in air-conditioned, pre-fab trailers for the sleeping quarters. Most of the people had little time to do anything else except work and sleep, and since no one ever visited the base, there was no reason to keep up appearances with other bases. And they hadn't.

Outside each of the barracks, rocks had been spread to give an even, landscaped feel to the living quarters, and to keep the sand from blowing around. Grass wouldn't grow, and the weeds that did still struggled through the spaces between the small rocks to find their way to light.

The bus stopped in front of the team's trailer and the twelve members entered their new home away from home. Inside, the trailer was subdivided into seven separate rooms that each slept two, with Colonel Mulgrave already taking the room at the end of the hall, near the kitchenette, for himself.

The rooms were your basic two bed, hotel-type rooms with a TV, desk, and shower. Chris decided to claim a room near the door and planned to grab the cooler bed away from the window and the sunlight. As he entered the room, he noticed that there was already someone thinking the exact same thing.

"Flip you for it." Chris said with a smile as he held out his hand. "Chris Ross."

"Mike Hecht." Mike said as he shook Chris's hand. "All right, you're on. I'll take heads."

Chris pulled a quarter from his pocket and flipped the coin covering it with his hand. As he looked at the result, he smiled. "How about best two out of three?"

Mike laughed, "That's okay, I'll take the other bed. Besides, it's closer to the air conditioning anyway."

Chris looked at Mike and smiled. "Deal."

Mike looked out the window at the view of sand, and then

turned to Chris. "Hey, you want to go check out the club and the rest of the base?"

"Sounds like a plan. I'll even buy you a beer for the bed."

Groom Lake was unique in the aspect that NCO's and Officers worked side by side, and because of the base's mission, there was only one club for both officers and enlisted. The Goatsucker Inn was nothing fancy, in keeping with the overall feeling of the rest of the base, just a bar with a few tables, TV, and juke box. If you wanted anything you had to get it yourself, or be nice to whoever was playing bartender.

Groom Lake was nothing if not practical. The base was dedicated to the missions that it served and not so much to the amenities afforded regular bases. Here the money went for the projects that were being tested and a few extra dollars each month for the extreme living conditions one had to endure to work here, but not much else.

The facilities weren't sparse, just not important. There was a room with a few weights and machines. Nothing fancy, but enough to get a good work out if that was your goal. Spartan was a theme that ran through the entire base. Everything on the base was functional, Chris and Mike realized, just not pretty. Everything here meant business.

5 GETTING READY

Every NCO of the two extraction teams trained in every aspect of rescue operations so that someone could always step in to do duties that were not necessarily theirs. The desert was perfect for receiving most of the additional training that the Colonel had ordered, however, not all of the training could be accomplished at Home Base and occasionally the team would be sent on what they affectionately called an educational vacation.

Such vacations included jump training for the SPs at Fort Benning, jungle training in Panama, swamp training in South Carolina and extensive Special Forces Small Unit Operation training at Fort Bragg, North Carolina. Each member had also been flown to Quantico, Virginia, where they received special training from the FBI's Hostage Rescue Team and a trip through the infamous paint house. Finally those who were not from the Pararescue career field were required to go through a specialized, more intimate version of the "pipeline". In a showing of team cohesiveness that had made the Colonel extremely happy, all members of the team opted to participate, even those who had already gone through the traditional Pararescue course.

The last additional training that the team received from an outside unit was Advanced Jump training where they were trained in HALO's or High Altitude, Low Opening jumps, and HAHO's, High Altitude, High Opening. Except for the pilots, the entire team was required to take this course, as it would also entail small team operations. For the Advanced Jump training, Colonel Mulgrave had brought the team back to Groom Lake and had called in a few favors with the brass in Washington to allow Master Sergeant Stuart Parker, a jump master from Fort Benning to come as a temporary duty assignment to do the instruction.

MSgt. Parker had grown up with Colonel Mulgrave, and after looking at the two of them you wondered if there was something in the water of their hometown. MSgt. Parker was actually bigger than his boyhood friend and for family or some other reason that Mulgrave couldn't quite figure out, and never really wanted to ask, had turned down an opportunity to play college football. Instead he had joined the Army. The 101st Airborne. He had joined them because at the time, in Stuart's mind, they had seemed the toughest. Sure there were the Green Berets and the Navy S.E.A.L.s, but to continuously jump from airplanes, with people shooting at you, that took balls. The funny thing was, he had actually enjoyed it, and after finding his way safely through Vietnam, he applied for, and was accepted to the Army's skydiving team, the Golden Knights.

With the number of jumps he had accumulated with the Golden Knights, and his talent for passing on to others the lessons that he himself had learned, his career was pretty much predetermined. With only the occasional diversion taking him away from Fort Benning, MSgt. Parker had become the most senior Master Jump Instructor in the Army. By all rights, he should have been behind a desk running the school, but due to his love of jumping and the lessons he knew he still could teach, he had managed on more than one occasion to pull a few strings and stay in the air instead of being tied to some desk in an office.

He used to joke to his friends that he taught because he got to push a lot of wet behind the ears, eighteen year old grunts out of perfectly good airplanes. But for all of the bravado, all of the ooorahs, he knew the real reason he taught the lesson plan developed for him by the Vietnamese years earlier and the importance of courage. He was teaching them to stick their fear into the pit of their stomach, bite their lip, and jump into harm's way. And he knew that if he could teach more of them how to do that without losing their nerve, and taught them the reasons why they jumped into that danger, maybe, just maybe more of them would make it home alive.

Because of this, the time it took to decide to do a favor for an old friend in the Air Force was seconds. He didn't know much more than the fact that he would be training a group of men who would comprise some sort of classified team. He didn't know what their mission would be. He didn't have to. All he needed to know was that they were black ops and that meant if they needed jump training, he could almost guarantee that they would see live combat. And his job, his passion, was to bring men like that home alive by giving them the best training that he had developed. He assumed, correctly, that since they were Air Force they would probably be some sort of rescue unit and that meant that they put themselves in harms way to bring someone else home. Someone in a place so terrible that normal teams wouldn't work. Slightly crazy, Stuart thought, but so was jumping out of perfectly good airplanes for the past twenty years.

For the Advanced Jump training the team temporarily moved to the Tonopah Air Base, since they had better facilities for their guest. Colonel Mulgrave had wanted the training to take place at Groom Lake, but the Base Commander and those higher up wanted to limit the exposure to Area 51, and with Tonopah a viable alternative they couldn't and didn't justify the risk of giving clearance to an Army instructor for just a few weeks training.

The team had no problem adapting to the facilities at Tonopah. The Pentagon had always planned on upgrading Tonopah to a full fledged base and had a few years before, began a three phase construction plan to bring the base amenities up to standard. The differences between Tonopah and Groom Lake were night and day.

The recreation center at Tonopah was state of the art, complete with baseball diamonds, a full gym with basketball, racquetball courts, and a stainless steel pool which struck Chris as a giant kitchen sink with a diving board. In fact, Mike and he had discussed the possibility of getting a giant scouring pad made in Las Vegas and placing it in the pool as a practical joke, but couldn't figure out how to get it up on the plane without sacrificing some of their much needed gear, or arousing suspicion and creating a practical joke war between the two sites.

Tonopah also had their own Officer's Club, the Tonopah Officers' Club and Chinese Laundry, which had started years earlier as a very small bar with a washer and dryer that the pilots had used as a gathering place. Now after the renovations, the bar was a full grown Officers' Club. Like any other bar in the world, the only difference being the old washer and dryer behind the bar and the name TOCACL, which was the acronym for the original name.

As with Groom Lake, the enlisted and officers worked closely together, and both groups were welcome at the bar where it was made clear that rank wasn't an issue. The club was an oasis in the middle of the Nevada high desert and Rescue Team Alpha spent a few off hours using their new oasis from training to get to know one another better. MSgt. Parker, however, kept a close eye on the team's bonding, knowing that nothing could slow down jump training faster than a bad hangover at forty thousand feet.

Chris loved the daytime jumps for it felt as if he could fall forever, although it felt more like flying than falling. As he fell through twenty-two thousand feet he realized that he was looking at what the gods originally meant only for the eyes of eagles. The desert spread out below him in a patchwork of different shades of brown. Below, a quilt of nature, and above the other members of the team. The exhilaration was amazing.

The temperature of the air at altitude was freezing cold even in the middle of summer, and Chris was thankful for the insulated suit that had previously been so uncomfortable. Chris looked at the webbed gloves on his hands and experimented with the different techniques that the team had gone over with MSgt. Parker on the ground. First he brought his arms in close to his side and closed his legs, becoming a bullet screaming at the earth at one hundred and fifty-six feet per second. Next he opened up to slow his rate of fall and extended his gloves so that the webbing caught the wind like a duck's foot catching water. Chris spent some time manipulating the air currents so that his body would change directions or positions and realized that freefalling was not unlike swimming through the moving air. Chris glanced at the altimeter on his wrist. The ride was almost over.

Below ten thousand feet the ground seemed to approach with amazing speed and Chris checked his altimeter. They were to open their parachutes at twenty-five hundred feet, and his altimeter read seventy-five hundred. Five thousand feet to go.

The desert below him seemed to be gaining speed. Chris could now see the bushes and other life that higher had appeared as slightly different hues of brown on the desert floor. With the return of his depth perception, he could make out the structures on the base clearly and see the trucks moving on the highway that cut through the desert. Chris again checked his altimeter and began to do his ritual request for the chute to open properly the first time. 3500, 3250, 3000, Chris grabbed the rip cord with his right hand, 2750, 2500, NOW! Chris pulled the rip cord. Immediately there was a ruffling and slight popping sound as his chute filled with air and the ground below seemed to reverse its course toward him. Chris looked above him where the other chutes opened in quick succession. The eight team members floated through the air like strangely painted military marionettes attached to canvas hands.

With experienced men you had to use different training tactics than with new recruits, you couldn't bully or intimidate them, and MSgt. Parker had discovered that while thoughts of mom and apple pie were nice a touch for Hollywood, money and beer worked best. NCOs would try to win at anything if the prize was either of those commodities and he had come upon a way to make things a bit more interesting and competitive on the jumps. Chris looked for his drop target and found that he was too far east. Damn, this one is going to cost big.

The bet was simple. For the first two jumps, it was a six pack for every ten feet away from the target, for jumps three through five it was for every five feet away, and for all jumps after five, including night jumps, it was per foot.

Chris watched the target with envy as the wind blew him farther east. This is going to be five six packs at least. Five if I'm lucky, Chris thought as his feet hit the sand sixty-five feet from target. When all of the team had landed and the measurements had been taken, it was discovered that there would be twenty-five new six packs in the beer account that night.

After the first couple of day jumps, MSgt. Parker had the team's Gulfstream and four pilots move to Tonopah for the duration of the training. Jumping out of the fast moving Gulfstream would be a very delicate operation, even in the best of conditions, and in his mind it was best that the team start learning how to do it as soon as possible.

The Gulfstream IV had been specially modified with advanced avionics, threat receivers and among other things a special hatch and pressurization systems in the rear compartment so that it could be opened in mid-flight. What appeared from the outside to be a normal maintenance access hatch, actually was a jump door that had been cut through the floor of the Gulfstream. Due to the speed of the Gulfstream, the pilot would have to slow the plane to just above stall speed to give the team a little relief from the three hundred mile per hour winds and jet wash that would attack their bodies as they exited the door. Even with the pilot's adjustment the team had to leave the hatch just right, and enter the jump in the proper position or risk serious injury. With thirty hours of simulated Gulfstream egresses already under their belts, MSgt. Parker felt it was now time to face the actual thing.

Chris looked across the desert and watched as the sun made the sky beyond the mountains to the east a pale shade of rose and wondered how morning always seemed to come so quickly. Today would be a live exercise having two of the pilots simulate bailing out over a hostile area, with half of the team acting in the role of aggressors. Each member would be wearing M.I.L.E.S. gear, a very advanced form of laser tag, to simulate actual combat and after the first team was finished the members would switch roles and the other team would jump. Chris made the short walk across the base to the dining facility as the rest of base slowly came alive.

Mike was already in line at the grill ordering a deluxe omelet with all of the trimmings as Chris grabbed a tray and slid next to him. The food at Tonopah was an unbelievable luxury, actually some of the best in the Air Force, and yet because of the secrecy of Tonopah the people who were stationed here would be the only ones to ever know that. Chris ordered a western omelet and caught up to Mike at the table.

"Do you believe this food?" Chris asked as he sat at the table and reached for the pepper.

"I guess they figure, you're out in the middle of the desert, they better feed you right." Mike replied.

"Well, an army travels on its stomach." Chris agreed as he lifted a slightly larger than normal bite of omelet off his plate and into the air, "Besides, where else are you going to go, McDonalds?" The rest of the team started to file into the chow hall and soon they were all gathered at the table, deeply engaged, not in the talk of tactics or strategy or even a second thought about the approaching exercise, but the very serious business of omelets.

The members separated into the two teams that they had been assigned to by Colonel Mulgrave. Team Two would be the first aggressor team, with Chris's Team One making the rescue, which made Chris happy since the black insulated jump suits would be almost unbearable during the later part of the afternoon, and they could take theirs off at the critique before they became the aggressors.

Team One waited until Team Two and the pilots were in position out in the Nevada desert and boarded the white Gulfstream to begin their rescue attempt. In this scenario, the two pilots had bailed out over one of the many deserts of the Middle East and were now on the ground, evading hostile forces.

The Gulfstream took off and streaked across the clear

morning sky as it climbed to thirty-five thousand feet, and the members of Team One prepared for their first jump out of the specially modified jet. Chris closed his eyes and tried to concentrate as MSgt. Parker's voice came over the radio inside his ear.

"Just a reminder gentlemen, the plane is going to be almost at a stall at the time of exit, so you really have to dive out and down once you leave the door. Everyone has to be out before the plane banks away and changes heading. If you don't make the thirty seconds, I'll stop you at the door, and the team will be one short going in. We're one minute out. Good luck."

Chris checked his gear, turned on his M.I.L.E.S. equipment, and secured his visor along with the other members of Team One as the pilot de-pressurized the rear of the cabin. Once the cabin pressure was stabilized MSgt. Parker opened the door and gave the thumbs up as the four members awaited the jump signal.

When the plane was just outside the drop zone the pilot pulled into a climb that brought the plane just this side of a stall. MSgt. Parker again gave the thumbs up and the order to jump came over the radio. Chris was first out the door and imagined in his mind's eye the other three members making the jump before the Gulfstream rolled right and left the area.

The members of Team One clustered together and started falling as a single unit, not four individuals, and entered the exercise as a team, each member doing his job with exacting precision. At about a thousand feet from the ground, Team One's M.I.L.E.S gear began beeping, signaling near misses by enemy fire. Suspended under a nylon canopy, feet not yet on the ground, with people shooting at you is not a pleasant experience and Chris realized that in real life this was not a theory he would want to test. Once on the ground, however, it became a different story. Now out of their vulnerable position, Team One became the aggressive unit, blending precise tactics and a few small surprises to cut off the hostile force and race to the downed pilots. When it was over Team One had rescued the two pilots, neutralized the hostile force, and the exercise was deemed a success.

After the critique and a brief rest to get water and lunch, the teams again separated and assumed the roles of rescuer and aggressor. This time Team One would be the aggressor to a very determined Team Two, and predictably, the outcome was the same. Since the two teams were equally matched, the tactics had been the one determining factor in the identical outcomes. At the end of the day, dirty and exhausted, but buoyed with the score, hostile forces: zero, good guys: two, Rescue Team Alpha returned to the Tonopah base to take a shower and spend the evening celebrating at TOCACL.

The next night the team assembled at 24:00 hours for a midnight or O-dark thirty jump. Cold, dark and quiet, this would be one of the most frightening things that Chris would ever go through. As frightening as combat is, at least you knew where the enemy was, or had a pretty good idea, but on a night HALO over the desert there was nothing out the back of the plane. Pure nothing. It was as if you were stepping off of your world into the eternal abyss. Because of this, the team went back to using the C-141 Starlifter. MSgt. Parker looked at the Security Police sergeants and wondered not who, but who he wouldn't have to push out of the plane tonight. It was a very rare thing indeed to have a person jump on his first night HALO, on his own accord, from forty thousand feet, without having anything visual to lock onto, or anything except the sound of your own oxygen and heart beat to keep you company.

The plane reached the jump altitude of forty thousand feet, and as it approached the drop zone everyone did one final check of their own and their buddy's gear. Chris wondered if everyone else was a tense as he was. He had jumped over fifty times but something about this seemed awkward. He tried to tell himself that he wasn't scared, but deep down inside he knew better. Without warning the green light went on and the back of the C-141 opened to a chasm of nothingness. MSgt. Parker was already at the rear of the plane barking for everyone to get up and get ready, yet Chris couldn't hear a thing, just saw his lips move in a surreal way. Chris again was to be the first out and as he approached the rear of the plane, he prepared to jump. Nothing but a walk in the park, Chris thought as he saw Parker give him the thumbs up. Chris stood in the rear of the plane, and didn't move. MSgt. Parker smiled and gave a little shake of his head as he casually walked up behind Sgt. Ross and pushed.

Chris re-orientated his body and focused his attention on the rest of the jump, there's no way in hell I'm going to owe as much as last time. Chris looked at the glowing numbers on the wrist altimeter and tried to see if he could get a glance at his target. Yeah right, you're 35,000 feet up, its dark, and you're over a desert, what the hell do you think you were going to see. There was complete nothingness. The only thing that gave Chris a sense of place was the pressure of the wind against his chest and the sound of the air from his own mask. He looked at his altimeter to verify that he was indeed falling, that he just didn't freeze in time when he, with a little help, had stepped out of the plane.

As much as he had enjoyed day jumps, this was going to take a little getting used to. He had jumped at night before, but at least you could see lights and from a lower altitude, you could see shapes and shadows. Here in the desert there were no lights, no shapes, no shadows, just blackness. Pure blackness. Chris couldn't wait until the next night jump when MSgt. Parker had promised the use of night vision goggles. This time, however, they were required to make the jump blind.

Chris glanced at his altimeter and noticed that he was already at ten thousand feet. Looking above Chris saw the stars of the night sky, and black spaces where there were no stars. He assumed that the spaces were the other members of the team. Chris returned his attention back to the jump as the beeping sound of his altitude indicator went off inside his earpiece. Chris again checked his altimeter. 5,000 feet. Time to get ready.

At five thousand feet the team spread apart to find their own targets. On this jump MSgt. Parker had placed eight individual targets and numbered each one through eight. He had briefed the team that each target was spaced a thousand feet from the others, and the location of each individual target. Then based on the wind direction and speed, they calculated their own chute openings so that they would be carried a different distance than their teammates.

To do this, however, they had to be apart at the time of

opening or it would be possible for one of the members to get tangled in the chute of another, ending in a horrific accident. For this reason, the team was wearing small flashing beacons that made them look like tiny airplanes with red lights on their arms. One by one the team members turned on their safety beacons, and from Chris's perspective it appeared to be a group of demonic fireflies.

Chris had calculated an opening altitude of four thousand feet, and started to separate from the team. At the same time the rest of the team were making their own adjustments in preparation for their openings. Chris looked around him to ensure that there were no lights around him, and being absolutely sure, checked his altitude one last time, said his prayer, and pulled the rip cord.

Again the chute filled with air, and the world came to a halt. The difference at night, since there were no visual references yet, was that the only sensation he could feel was the swinging motion of the harness. Chris had overestimated that he would see his target at around three thousand feet. He was already through three thousand and couldn't make out a thing. Glancing around he noticed that the safety beacons were spread out and staggered in the night sky. Turning his attention back to the ground he could just start making out subtle changes in the blackness. Chris imagined that the changes in color were ground shapes, but just couldn't be sure. It was like walking down the stairs with your vision blocked, where you thought you had made the last step, but there was still one more. The kind of stagger that you get in your heart when you find that last step, and almost go head over heals.

Chris's heart was going a thousand miles an hour as he

floated through fifteen hundred feet. There! That must be it. The circle was too perfect to be anything but the target. The problem was he was still too far away for the altitude he was at, and unless the wind increased in speed, Chris would owe more to the beer fund. At least not as much as the last jump, Chris smiled, Maybe only two six packs.

The ground popped into Chris's vision unexpectedly, it just kind of materialized around one hundred feet, and by the time Chris had prepared to land, it was there. Even though he had bent and rolled to absorb the shock, the force of the landing shuddered through Chris's body, right through his spine to the top of his head.

Chris marked his landing spot with a glow stick and went to the recovery area to join the rest of the team. After a few moments of bullshitting with the others the sound of MSgt. Parker's voice came from the recovery vehicle, "Looks like three six's Ross."

"TWO!" Chris replied.

"Are you doubting my measuring abilities, Sergeant?"

"Not at all Sarge, I just thought in your advancing years, you might be getting a little rusty."

MSgt. Parker laughed, "All right Chris, nice jump, I'll let you off with two. By the way, you didn't happen to call me a mother fucker did you."

Chris looked at the rest of the team. "Busted", Chris said as he loaded his chute into the back of the Jimmy.

"That's all right, you should have heard what Sgt. Hoffman called me."

"What do you expect, going around throwing people out of flying airplanes, you're lucky we don't take you with us." Chris jumped into the back of the Jimmy and used the rolled chutes as a makeshift bed.

"It's what I get paid for kids, ain't America great?" MSgt. Parker grinned as he put the Jimmy in gear and drove off into the night.

MSgt. Parker pulled the Jimmy up to the security check point at Tonopah and handed the guard his ID and was waved through, but instead of going back to the barracks he pulled the vehicle into the parking lot of the recreation center. "It's tradition that after your first night HALO, the person that threw you out of the plane buys you a drink. And that, gentlemen, would be me."

Once inside TOCOCAL, the team realized that there was something more going on than a round of traditional drinks. As the team entered the darkened room, the voice of Colonel Mulgrave came from the center. "Please, gentlemen, form a circle." The team, as instructed, formed a circle around Colonel Mulgrave, joined by the four pilots, as MSgt. Parker went behind the bar and poured fourteen shots of tequila, handing one to each member of the team.

"Each of you tonight has made the jump into the proverbial abyss. You have looked at nothing and stepped into it. You have come soaring out of the night sky to land safely again on earth.

MSgt. Parker and I talked about the importance of having, however small, some sort of ritual for this moment when it came, and so tonight, we are here. As of tonight, you have made it through all of the additional training that I developed. The only thing left is to perfect these skills, but you all have made it through the hardest part. Tonight, you are officially a team. Together you have flown and together you will fly.

"As commander of this team, I have decided on a name more fitting than the generic 'Rescue Team Alpha'. As of this moment, we will be known as the Nighthawks. Born out of darkness, bringing others to light, our motto will be Courage, Honor, Duty." Colonel Mulgrave paused and raised his glass in toast. "Gentlemen. To courage, honor, and duty."

As one the group responded and raised their glasses.

"To courage, honor, duty. Nighthawks — ooorah!"

The cheer brought a smile to MSgt. Parkers face. He now knew more of their mission than when he had first accepted the assignment and he realized that if he was ever in a jam, like that of a pilot shot down behind enemy lines, he could take comfort in the knowledge that this team existed. Unfortunately he also knew that pilots wouldn't learn of this team, until the time for that comfort had passed. That was a shame he thought, but knew that it was necessary.

The Nighthawks downed their shots and Colonel Mulgrave handed each a small box.

"Due to the nature of our unit, and since we don't wear patches on our uniforms, I thought that these would be appropriate. Wear them in health."

Each member opened his box, finding inside a unit signet ring. Cast in gold, each had placed in the center a black onyx stone in which was carved in gold a descending hawk, wings outstretched, holding red lightning bolts in its talons. On the inside the team's motto was inscribed: Courage. Honor. Duty.

6 RELATIONSHIPS

After Jump training ended the two teams of the Nighthawks, started their normal routine of four days on and four days off. Since the two teams rotated, they didn't usually work with each other, unless there was an exercise or an emergency that would require them to combine forces, and a competition formed between the two smaller units. A testosterone driven competition for bragging rights over which team was sharper, better, stronger. In some ways the competition provided the drive to make yourself better than you were the day before. Which when you are in a career that occasionally has people shooting at you, is not such a bad thing, but it also made the Nighthawks feel like two smaller, separate units.

The four days spent at Groom Lake were pretty routine. You arrived early in the morning the first day of your tour and went to roll call to get the duty roster. Then you would work on ways to make the equipment better or the technique or yourself. Then there were the hours spent in the gym. The constant pursuit to become stronger and kill spare time. Each team member usually worked out two or three hours a day. After the gym there was TV and sleep, and a few old video games, then up at the crack of dawn to do it all again.

The four days off, however, were a different story. Las Vegas was a very accommodating town, and with the mountains and Lake Mead, there was always something to do. Chris's team usually found themselves spending almost as much off-time together as they did on work days, and Chris found himself developing a friendship with his roommate and Team One's leader Mike Hecht.

Chris and Mike both liked rock climbing and hiking and their similar interests brought them together more than the rest of the team. Usually, when they had the time, Chris and Mike would sneak off to the canyons right outside of Las Vegas and climb some of the more challenging cliffs. The cliffs became a place to find out about each other. And both had discovered that the rocks were therapeutic as the challenge that they provided brought out the best in both men. Both of them being risk takers, they discovered that each one thrived when things became the most challenging. And each would go out of their way to help the other. There on the face of the red cliffs, one hundred feet above the ground, their friendship was tempered and steeled. At the summit they would end up having long talks about philosophy, the way that each saw life, and over the specific requirements of their original career field, Mike's Pararescue which dealt with medical rescue in hostile environments or Chris's Security Police E.S.T. which handled hostage rescue in urban areas.

Mike's views on life were very black and white. Things to him were either right or wrong, no questions asked, no gray area. To Chris there were definitely gray areas, even many shades of gray within those areas and there was very little in this world that was actually black and white. It surprised Chris that someone so different from himself, in so many ways, could in some ways, seem cut from the same cloth.

This morning the sun was shining through the bright blue sky with its usual intensity as Mike and Chris drove out of Las Vegas to the dark red rocks just outside of town. The cliff that was chosen this morning, was not overly challenging but enough to give the two a serious workout. Because of youthful feelings of invincibility, both climbed without ropes.

Today Chris made the mistake of letting Mike lead. A mistake he soon regretted. Mike was only three inches taller than Chris, but when you're reaching for a finger hold, three inches can make the difference between a hold and being stuck on the face of a rock wall with the muscles in your legs starting to tremble. Most of the times it had happened today, Chris had worked his way out of the dead ends. This one was different. Chris grabbed the rock with every ounce of strength left in his fingers.

"You coming up, or are you going to wait for a bus?" Mike asked as he peered over the top at his friend below.

"Actually I thought I'd stay here awhile to enjoy the thrill." Chris replied as he started looking for another way to get to the summit, the muscles in he calves starting to shake. Chris had learned that if you reached a certain area, no matter how stuck you were, there was always a way out. In some ways the thought was calming, almost eastern in its spirituality; in other ways, it was maddening. The more you tried to calm your nerves and focus, the more the muscles in your arms and legs started to shake, causing the panic that started in the pit of your stomach to move to the extremities, which caused your brain to try and calm the body even more, resulting in an endless loop that usually fatigued the climber to the point of danger.

Chris looked around at the handholds that were almost within his reach. He could try to go down, but Chris hated the thought of going down the mountain blind.

"Mike, I might need a hand. It appears that I am momentarily detained." Chris smiled as his friend looked over the top of the cliff.

"Oh just admit it, you're stuck." Mike said as he got down on his stomach and looked over the edge to find a hand hold for his friend.

Chris took a deep breath and looked again at the rock face in front of him. Above and to the left of him, just out of reach was a hold that would lead to another, and another, taking him to the top. He would have to stretch more than would be safe at this height, but the more he stayed here on the cliff, the more fatigued his body would become, increasing the chance of a fall. Chris made sure his foothold was secure, and stretched. Barely, at the very edges of his fingertips, lightly grazing the pads, was the hold. Chris stretched with every muscle in his body.

Mike looked over the edge of the cliff and saw that his friend was stretched out as far as possible, not really on the foothold he had been using, nor, on the new handhold, just in a point of space between the two, taking the risk that the new hold would work.

For a few brief moments, Chris felt the strange sensation of being on the rock, but not really holding on to anything, just barely remaining on the proper side of falling.

And in a moment it was over. His hand had found the new hold and he easily made the rest of the climb to the top.

Chris looked at Mike and smiled. "I told you I wasn't stuck."

Mike shook his head as he reached in the backpack and pulled out a canteen of water and took a swig before handing it to Chris. "You know, maybe we should carry ropes and stuff in here." Both men looked at each other, laughed, and answered at the same time, "Nah."

There was a path up the back of the canyon that didn't have any cliffs and occasionally Mike's wife, Sarah, would join them at the top and the three of them would sit and watch the distant lights of Las Vegas until late in the night.

Team One also had a weekly golf outing. All four sergeants of the team played golf and therefore always had a foursome, and almost always played a game of skins. One exception to the Colonel's rules about being on the base was the course at Nellis AFB where the team usually played. It was less of a golf course, and more like strips of grass in the middle of a sand box. And that was unfortunate because the team played golf more off of the fairway than on and that meant that a good portion of time was devoted to chasing balls through the sand and Joshua trees.

Chris stepped up to the first tee and prepared to drive. The hole was a slight dog-leg right with a pond bordering one side and the ever present desert on the other. 21 Left, one of the runways at Nellis was directly in view of the tee-box, and the landing F-15's, F-16's and various other jets, gave the hole a feeling of a very large miniature golf course, complete with animated obstacles.

Chris looked at his alignment and started his backswing, stopping just at the right moment before shifting his weight forward and turning his hips for the downswing. Being the first teeing off for the foursome, Chris had wanted to make a drive that would leave the others in awe, and as his club approached the ball, he was sure this was going to be the one.

At the moment the clubface made contact with the ball, there was a soft popping sound and the round object that had once been a golf ball on Chris's tee, was now a white cloud of dust blowing in the desert breeze.

The other three members could barely control their laughter at the prank as others waiting to tee off had a definite air of non-amusement.

Mike smiled a devilish smile and raised his eyebrows. "Gotcha."

Chris shook his head and reached into his pocket to replace the exploded ball, not even acknowledging the practical joke, just giving a look that the two of them knew meant that, sometime, somewhere, someday, he would get his revenge. And when he did, it would be worth the wait.

They played each week and usually ended up at Mike's house to be pampered by Sarah. With the exception of the pilots, Mike Hecht was the only one of Team One's members that was married. The others ejoyed the freedom of being single in Las Vegas. Most of the guys dated occasionally, but with what they did, and the hours that they kept, it was hard to get serious with anyone in particular, and in a way each envied Mike for the stability of always having someone to come home to.

They had been high school sweethearts and Sarah had become a favorite of the rest of the team. Blonde, beautiful, and with a heart as big as the state in which she and Mike grew up, she had hospitality down to an art form. At least once a month and sometimes more, Sarah would dig out an old family recipe and cook up a real down-home, southern Texas barbecue. Chris was always amazed at the time she spent searching for just the right cut of meat, or just the right spices, and just the right beer, which lately had come from the units' beer fund. Occasionally Colonel Mulgrave, or one of the pilots would make it to one of the Hecht's gatherings, which had an open invitation, but usually they remained to themselves, spending the few precious days off with their own families.

The Hecht family, Mike and Sarah, to the curiosity of their neighbors, had built a barbecue pit with a fifty gallon oil drum cut in half. The aroma from the cooking meat would send the rest of the neighborhood out to the local store to grab some steaks and fire up the grill. Mike would send away to a mail order firm in Texas for fresh mesquite or hickory instead of charcoal, and the neighborhood would be filled with not only the smell of charcoal, but the sweet smell of a real Texas hardwood barbecue.

Sarah would begin early in the morning, marinating the meat, and while the boys went out to the golf course to lose a few balls, she would start the fire and cook the meat until they came home. Dinner would be served about three o'clock, family style, which Chris found out was a cute Texas way of saying "everybody for themselves" or "don't put your hand in front of my fork", and would end sometime around whenever.

Five people who didn't know anyone in a strange town, in a strange state, and in a strange circumstance used these barbecues to become closer than they had been with anyone else in their lives. Sharing themselves in that way that only those whose lives depended on each other, day in and day out could.

7 FINALS

Colonel Mulgrave entered the briefing room and closed the door behind him. The other members of the Nighthawks were already in their seats, trying desperately to figure out what the Colonel had up his sleeve. The Colonel looked at the men seated in front of him and wondered if they were up to the task that he had arranged with General Mitchell. They were the best when you found them, and you've given them almost a year of training, they can handle it.

The Colonel cleared his throat and looked again at the men he had personally selected. He had searched for them, watched them train, went to bat for them and now put their, and his, reputation on the line. He knew every idiosyncrasy, every personality quirk, every strength and weakness. He knew this team better than he knew himself, and now was the time to prove it.

"Gentleman, I know for the last few weeks you have heard me talk about a final exam. I know that you have all probably speculated about what it is and that you all have your own personal theories, and I am here to tell you that they are all wrong."

Colonel Mulgrave reached into his briefcase and pulled out twelve exercise mission packets. "MSgt. Parker and I have spoken, and we both feel that you are ready to do what you've been trained for. The exercise will commence as soon as I leave this room, and the five of you that are married should notify your wives that you won't be home as scheduled. Inside your mission folders you will find everything that you need to successfully complete the mission.

"General Mitchell, MSgt. Parker, and I will be observing the progress of the team, but will not be able to provide assistance in any way. Everything will be done as it would if this were real, except that all of your communications with Home Base will be simulated by contacting me on the radio when you make the jump and when you complete the mission. Those should be the only times that you will need to contact Home Base, and if it isn't, just fake it.

"Before I leave and start the exercise, I just want to say this. Both MSgt. Parker and I feel that you are all more than ready for this challenge. If not, I wouldn't have accepted it. It's going to be hard, it's going to be hell, and it's going to look impossible, so forget what you're looking at and think you see, and do as you're trained. I'll see you at the other end."

Colonel Mulgrave closed his briefcase, gave one final look at the team assembled in front of him, and smiled. "Good luck Nighthawks." They're ready was the only thought that went through his mind as he opened the door and stepped into the role of observer.

Inside the packets were all of the answers to the thousands

of questions that were going through the minds of the Nighthawks. The overall objective for the team was to enter a heavily defended area without being detected, arrive at a predetermined location, retrieve a special flag, and get out. Their objective: The interior of a mock base located in the woods of North Carolina defended by the 3rd SOG, the same unit that had trained them in small unit operations. They had four days to complete the mission and could use any means necessary, using any resources that they could find.

The mission packets also contained photographic intelligence of the mock base as well as the frequencies that the aggressors would be using. Everything that the CIA or the NSA would provide if this were an actual mission. Everything that the Nighthawks would need to know to take advantage of any weakness.

As he would on a real mission involving both teams, SSgt. Hecht was Nighthawk team leader. He looked around the room and could already see the gears in his team members' heads turning.

"All right people listen up. The first thing that I want to hear from you are any ideas on getting in there. From there we'll create a plan of rescue and egress. Start talking."

"I have an idea!" Chris answered with mock seriousness. "We could parachute in."

SSgt. Hecht threw the pen that was in his hand at his friend, hitting him square in the chest. "Brilliant. Okay everyone, it has now been proven beyond a reasonable doubt that Chris Ross, Sergeant USAF, does indeed have a brain. A very small one, but definitely a brain." Laughter filled the briefing room as the rest of the Nighthawks started pelting Chris with various small objects.

SSgt. Hecht moved to the chalkboard at the front of the room. "Seriously people, let's have some ideas." Silence filled the room as the members of the team became serious and started pouring over their mission packets. Staring off into space, they let their imaginations take over the thinking process. Since the 3rd SOG trained them, they would know, or assume to know, the moves that the Nighthawks would make. For that reason every member of the team knew the importance of coming up with a very creative, very outrageous plan, that no one would expect.

It was the main guiding principle of the Nighthawks, and other than rescue techniques was considered most important by Colonel Mulgrave. It was the reason he had decided on such a relatively small team. If every member could improvise on their own, knowing the overall objective and what the others of the team would probably do, if there was ever a problem or failure on one part of the team, it wouldn't destroy the rest. That philosophy was carried even to the group level so that the team as one would improvise, making the job of the enemy that much more difficult.

SSgt. David Miller looked at the recon photos that were in the mission packet as a plan started to formulate in his head. "Mike, I might have something." The rest of the Nighthawks listened to his idea, adding bits and pieces, changing this and that, until they had a plan that they all believed would work.

The plan was simple really, the hardest and most important thing would be timing the chute openings so that they would be close enough to the fields to make out the trees from the lower altitude without much difficulty.

There was a large field to the north of camp that the Rangers would watch, expecting it to be the main landing site.

The two Nighthawks that were the best in evasion would land there and when needed provide a distraction by showing enough of themselves to be seen, but not enough to make it look obvious. The rest of the team would split into two man teams and land at smaller more dangerous sites that circled the camp. They would hike the mile to their objective and enter the compound, meeting at the predetermined spot, the recreation room right below the observation tower.

The mission packets also had a picture of their rescue objective, a small red and white flag that would be placed in the center of the camp. The Nighthawk's plan called for them to bring a duplicate flag to swap with the original to give them some much needed time.

The team decided to time their approach flight so that they would be over the drop zone at 04:00 hours. The most difficult time to stay alert if you have been awake all night, which would be an advantage that the Nighthawks would exploit by sleeping on the flight and being rested before going in. Everything was in place. The team would depart at 23:00 hours the following night. Until then they were to take care of their uniforms and get as much rest as possible.

At 23:00 hours on the second night of the exercise, the white Gulfstream climbed into the night sky above Groom Lake and headed east across the sleeping country. In the observation tower of the compound Colonel Mulgrave, MSgt. Parker, the Army's special forces team leader, Captain Peters, stood staring out at the North Carolina night. General Mitchell was back in Washington, due to other situations that demanded his attention, but left strict orders to contact the communication center at the Pentagon whenever anything happened. He wanted this to simulate a real mission down to the smallest detail, even if it meant waking him up in the middle of the night.

During the least likely times of attack the other three men took turns resting in the recreation room below, but now at three in the morning, all were in the tower watching the movements of the defender force. The protection plan that the Captain had come up with was indeed formidable. He had listening and observation teams hidden every fifty meters around the camp, with two man teams in each of the four towers that were on the corners. There was a thirty foot section of clear zone surrounding the camp from the fence to the trees that had infrared lights. These protected the defenders' night vision while illuminating the area to the special cameras feeding into the command center. And on top of all this were the random patrols that were continuously moving.

Colonel Mulgrave looked at the fence and nodded his head. "Nice job with the defenses Captain. You're really going to give my team a challenge."

"With all do respect sir, your Air Force wannabes don't stand a chance against my men. Remember, we taught them everything they know."

Well not everything you smug little asshole. Colonel Mulgrave thought as the muscles in his jaw tightened. MSgt. Parker watched as the rage entered his friend's body and then subsided as silence again encroached the tower. Little did the Captain know that even though he himself was Army, inside he was desperately waiting for those so called wannabes to kick some arrogant Army ass.

Thirty minutes out from the drop zone the Nighthawks started waking from their naps and began to check their gear for the upcoming jump. They would jump in four two man teams, with Chris and Mike being team two. Since there would be radio silence each of the team members switched their radios to the scanner frequency so that they could listen to the radio traffic of the 3rd SOG, and hear what was happening thirty thousand feet below.

The copilot came back and gave the signal for everyone to put on their air packs as he de-pressurized the rear cabin to prepare for the jump. Chris looked at his watch and noticed that they had picked up a tail wind and were five minutes ahead of schedule, as the coolness of the fresh oxygen touched his cheek. Mike checked Chris's chute and turned around for him to do the same.

The copilot opened the rear door and gave the thumbs up to the Nighthawks, wishing them luck as the light in the back cabin turned green. Within thirty seconds all of the members of Rescue Team Alpha were screaming towards the earth and four pinpoint targets in the North Carolina country. After the teams were out of the plane, the pilot called the simulated Home Base and confirmed that the teams were in by asking for a weather check on the wrong frequency. Below on the ground Colonel Mulgrave and MSgt. Parker smiled at each other as the Army Captain looked on at his defenses. Colonel Mulgrave excused himself and went to make a phone call to the Pentagon.

In Washington a phone rang in the bedroom of General Mitchell. His wife, wakened, just handed Paul the phone.

"General Mitchell, it's Sgt. Davis, Com Center sir. We just

received notification that exercise Team Strength has begun." The voice on the other end of the phone said, not at all bothered that they had interrupted the General's sleep.

"Very well, have my driver pick me up immediately."

"Yes sir, we already dispatched the driver. He should be there in five minutes."

"Thank you Sergeant." General Mitchell hung up the phone and rolled over to tell his wife that he was going to the office. His wife just continued sleeping on her side and Paul couldn't tell if she was really sleeping or silently cursing the job that continued to drag him out of her arms at night. Probably the latter. Paul took his clothes into the bathroom so that he could change without bothering her.

When he arrived at his office in the Pentagon, there was already a pot of coffee put on by the night shift and General Mitchell poured himself a cup of the thick, black, hearty liquid. Yes, hearty was a polite way to describe it thought Paul. Very hearty. Where are the Navy guys when you need them. Now they know how to make a decent pot of coffee. As Paul took a brave sip of the liquid, Sergeant Davis brought the thermal image from satellite SB1B-7 over to General Mitchell's desk.

"Sir, this is the image from SB1B-7, which the NSA sortied over the exercise location. We have both real frame, and thermal. I thought that you would be more interested in the thermal."

"How long ago was this taken" asked General Mitchell.

"Fifteen minutes, sir."

"Thank you Sergeant, I'll call you if I need to." The Sergeant placed the photos on the General's desk and left the office. General Mitchell sat down in his chair, took another distasteful sip of coffee, and opened the envelope.

Chris and Mike landed right on target and immediately camouflaged their chutes in the dirt and leaves. As quickly as they had appeared out of the night sky, they were gone, disappearing into the North Carolina woods without a trace. Quickly and quietly the two moved towards their objective and reached a bluff overlooking the camp. Now is where it got tricky, and extremely time consuming. Both knew that there would be listening posts, the trick was to find them first and then avoid them.

Chris scanned the area with his night vision goggles looking for anything that would disclose the location of their opponent. It had taken a while but they had discovered and mapped the location of each L.P. between them and the camp. Due to the lack of radio traffic from the Rangers, it could be properly assumed that they had yet to be discovered.

Once inside the perimeter of the listening/observation posts the only thing that they had to worry about were the random patrols and entering the camp. Mike scanned the fence line of the mock base and cursed. "Damn. They have infrared in the clear zone. Any ideas on blocking the sensors?"

Chris thought for a moment while he too scanned the fence. "Maybe we don't have to Mike, look three meters to the left of the second sensor." Chris directed Mike's vision to a drainage tunnel that came from the interior of the camp. "If we could get to the tunnel, we're in."

Both men smiled at each other and again disappeared into

the North Carolina night, becoming barely perceptible spirits, the tunnel now their new objective. The two members of the Nighthawks reached the storm ditch on their stomachs and looked inside. The tunnel was big enough to get through on your stomach, but was protected by steel reinforcement bars at the entrance. Mike reached out and grabbed one of the bars. "Any more ideas?"

Chris smiled and reached around to a black fanny pack that he wore under his regular issued gear packs. "Welcome to Felix's magic bag of tricks."

Mike smiled. "You've been watching to much MacGyver on cable Chris. What 'cha got in there?"

"Oh just something you can get at your local hardware store." Chris pulled out a twelve inch wire saw that had rings on either end. "It slices, it dices, it chops and cuts." Chris smiled. "Actually it's a carbide blade that will cut through just about anything. Rock, cement, metal, and its specialty, tunnel bars that piss off Nighthawks."

Mike shook his head. "Remind me to watch more MacGyver."

The three observers stood in the observation tower and searched the night for any signs of movement. "You know," the Captain started, "I hope your boys do come tonight. We have a few surprises up our sleeves for 'em." Captain Peters smirked. "Why doesn't the Air Force just stick to flying planes and leave the ground work to the professionals."

The muscles in Colonel Mulgrave's jaw again tightened, causing his teeth to grind slightly as he began to speak. "With all do respect Captain, I've had about all of those comments that I care to hear. I personally chose these men for their abilities, and with your training those abilities became even greater. So please, just keep your comments to yourself until the conclusion of the exercise. Understood?"

The Captain turned towards MSgt. Parker, expecting an ally, and smirked. "Yes sir, colonel."

The storm drain's exit was in the center of the compound under the observation tower, luckily hidden from view from just about every angle except directly above. Chris and Mike exited the drain and melted into their surroundings to listen. There was nothing except the occasional voice of a defending force member checking in with their leader to tell them all was secure. If they only knew, Chris thought.

The two Nighthawks made their way around the edge of the recreation center and positioned themselves below the window that was closest to the tower. Again reaching into his bag of tricks Chris pulled out a small dental mirror on a telescoping rod and peered through the window.

Inside two Rangers were taking a break watching TV and having coffee to stay awake. Chris communicated to Mike with hand signals that the room contained two and that they were stationed by the far wall. Mike nodded and gave the signal to move towards the door and take the two Rangers by surprise. Fortunately their night vision would be shot from the TV and they wouldn't be able to see into the night beyond the doorway.

Chris and Mike entered through the open doorway and slowly made their way deeper into the room. Due to the late hour and the lack of stimulus, the two Rangers were totally focused on the TV and barely noticed the hint of movement from the corner of the room. By the time they did notice it was too late. As they focused on Chris in the corner of the room, Mike came up from behind and declared both of them "dead".

Under the rules of the exercise, if you were "dead" you were bound by honor not to make a sound to notify your fellow teammates, so both Rangers dutifully surrendered their weapons and sat back down to watch TV.

Chris marked the outside door of the recreation room with ink that was visible only through night vision goggles, to let the other Nighthawks know that the building was secure. But instead of marking the top center of the door frame, which was standard practice for most military teams, Chris marked the lower right corner, a mark that would only be visible by those looking directly for it. Something the Nighthawks had decided upon before they had left the safety of Groom Lake. Something the Rangers wouldn't expect. When that was completed Chris sat with the two Rangers and waited for the rest of the team as Mike went out to replace the flag.

The night in the tower was becoming long and tedious as MSgt. Parker looked out over the darkened camp and wondered if the Nighthawks were even close. Out of the corner of his eye he caught the slight movement of the target flag, and the almost imperceptible hint of a shadow moving along the far building. MSgt. Parker smiled. Damn if they didn't do it. Parker caught the eye of Colonel Mulgrave, nodded, and smiled. Both men now knew that the team was inside and had completed the first part of the mission.

Colonel Mulgrave cleared his throat, much more relaxed, and looked out over the defended fields. "Captain, about what you were saying before, about my men being wannabes, would you like to make a wager on it?"

The smile on the Captain's face went from ear to ear, and

the Colonel could tell the thought going through the arrogant little prick's mind. Like taking candy from a baby, Mulgrave thought as he looked directly into the Captain's smug eyes.

"You gotta a deal Colonel, what's the bet?"

"Two hundred."

"Dollars?" asked the Captain, "that's a bit steep isn't it?"

"Not dollars, Captain, gambling's illegal. Push ups."

MSgt. Parker let out a slight laugh. He couldn't wait to see the Captain face down in the dirt counting out each one.

The Captain held out his hand. "I hope your boys can do two hundred sir."

"Oh, I wouldn't worry too much about that." Colonel Mulgrave smiled as he shook the Captain's hand and winked at MSgt. Parker.

Mike re-entered the rec center and waited with Chris for the rest of the team to arrive. The other two teams arrived at the center within ten minutes and proceeded to empty the refrigerator of all the sodas. Once the Nighthawks had drank their fill of the Ranger's refrigerator they started changing into the uniforms that they had brought with them and in minutes the entire room was filled with impostor Rangers. SSgt. Mike Hecht changed frequencies on his radio and sent out the coded message that would tell the distraction team to do their stuff, and looked at the rest of the team. "There's been a slight change guys. Chris and I entered through a storm drain right around the corner. We should exit that way and then make for the tree line. Any disagreement?"

The rest of the Nighthawks shook their heads and gathered their gear for the trip out. Almost immediately the radios of the Rangers erupted with the discovery of movement out near the tree line and the camp jumped to life.

Mike looked at Chris and nodded. "Gentleman, I believe that's our wake up call, let's dance."

In the observation tower, the Army Captain jumped to the side that reported the movement and watched as his team converged on the area only to find an empty field, and the call from another observation post that someone has been seen in sector three.

As the Rangers chased the phantom teams, the rest of the Nighthawks crawled through the drainage tunnel and again melted into the surrounding area, sending one last message to Colonel Mulgrave, "We're clear and out of here, mission accomplished, no casualties. Score one for the good guys." Colonel Mulgrave looked at the Captain still chasing the diversion team and smiled. The number two hundred was very fine indeed.

8 DOWNED

Five minutes from the coast of North Korea, Colonel Hammer brought the Raptor to an altitude of fifty feet above the cold dark Sea of Japan and turned on the LANTRN system. At fifty feet he would be sure to miss any other air traffic in the area and the computer plotted course created from the satellite images would keep him away from any heavily populated areas. He might buzz a farm house, but at night they would probably think it was one of their own and if they complained, by the time anyone would know different, Sledge would be having a beer in Hawaii.

A simple milk run Sledge thought, get in, get the photos, and beat feet back to the friendlies. It was odd that as many times in his career as he had made a trip exactly like this one, Vietnam, Honduras, and Cuba, it never got any less intense. He never lost that strange feeling in the pit of his stomach, like maybe one of these times the other side would get lucky with the golden BB. One lucky shot that hit you no matter what you did. No matter what kind of superstitious ritual you had performed, or what kind of rabbit's foot you carried.

Colonel Hammer checked the LANTRN system and watched as the coast of North Korea slipped under his wings. Here we go Sledge, hostile territory. He turned his attention back to the LANTRN system. Modern technology was a marvel, if not a bit unnerving. Here was a veteran combat pilot, now relinquishing control of his airplane to a computer. Well not total control, Sledge thought. He could at anytime override the system, but pilots who did that at low altitudes usually didn't come home to tell about it. It was a question of trust. Sure, they didn't fail very often, but what if?

Sledge watched the computer make course corrections as the Raptor screamed above the tree tops. He could never do this manually. If he tried, by the time the nerve impulses from his brain traveled to the muscles to correct an action, the mountain in front of him would be his final resting place. The map on his display showed the target point one hundred miles north of his current position and approaching quickly. At this pace, he thought, I'll be having a cold one by dawn.

The target came into view, ahead and slightly to the left, a small, well hidden, nuclear weapons storage facility. Colonel Hammer turned off the LANTRN and eased the stick a little to the left. He aligned with the target and pressed the trigger on his joystick. If this had been war, a bomb would have been released from the weapons bay and be falling towards the target. This time, however, it would only be the shutter of a very high speed, powerful camera.

The people on the ground looked up at the noise from above, and scurried about to notify their superiors about the unauthorized aircraft flying over their location. It was unmistakably NOT North Korean.

Now will be the hard part, thought Sledge, they know I'm

here and will be looking for me all of the way home. Colonel Hammer again turned on the LANTRN device and egressed the area.

Fresh from training and a little to nervous to do a good job, Private Yi Hu-Sun was at the radar of SAM Site 7. It was more of a fluke than anything. The blip came on his screen just barely, not even a blip really, more like a ghost signature, but something. Private Yi Hu-Sun looked around for his superior to get guidance on what he should do next, but he was out of the control center having a cigarette. Without the advice of someone more experienced, Private Yi Hu-Sun picked up the phone and called the units in the area closest to the blip, to have them look out just in case. It could be a test, thought Hu-Sun. He had heard that they do that to Privates all the time, and if you failed you were sent back to the infantry. By the time his supervisor came back to inform him in a very unfriendly way that he was just an ignorant, wet-behind-the-ears rookie, that all he had seen was a flock of birds on the radar screen, that because of him soldiers were running around chasing after wild geese, the message had been received and copied. The Sergeant picked up the phone to belay the order and recall the units chasing the flock, but stopped. Screw them. It would do them good to get a little exercise tonight, he thought with a smile as he hung up the phone. If you don't like running around, then you shouldn't be in the infantry.

As the call from the command center went out to all ground troops in a hundred mile radius of the blip, ten thousand North Korean Army personnel looked to the sky.

Colonel Hammer watched again as the LANTRN made a course adjustment and headed for the third waypoint. The

LANTRN was working with uncanny precision as it guided the F-22 through the mountains and into a canyon that was only one hundred meters wide. As far as he could tell, he was still running clean with no spikes on his threat indicator. Fifteen more minutes of hell, thought Sledge. Just like the old fighter pilot saying, "hours of pure boredom, followed by a few moments of shear terror." Fifteen more minutes until he was feet wet over the Sea of Japan.

Sergeant Kim Hyong-Tae and his Stinger missile unit were on routine patrol in the southern mountains of their homeland, and had it not been for the canyon funneling and amplifying sounds in their direction, they probably never would have heard the approaching aircraft. It was the unmistakable sound of a jet engine traveling at a very low altitude. This could be a promotion, Sergeant Kim thought, I have to do this one right. Finding a clearing, Sgt. Kim told his men to spread out fifty meters apart, and had them all arm their Stinger missiles and shoulder-launched heat seeking missiles. He knew that they would only get one chance at this and it could mean the difference between being a hero, or a scapegoat. "Whoever hits the intruder will get a two day pass." Sgt. Kim yelled to his men. That should get their attention. His men had spread out and were in a line across the only way out of the valley. "Turn on your radar and actively scan the area, you won't have much time once the intruder comes over that ridge."

Colonel Hammer came out of the canyon and into a clearing between the mountains. Again he checked his threat indicator and looked at his time estimate until he was feet wet. Only seven more minutes, thought Sledge. As he screeched over the valley he could see movement on the ground below. Usually that would have worried him, but the only thing that could touch him now, on no notice, was the infamous golden BB, and tonight, that just wasn't going to happen.

Sgt. Kim watched as the dark shadow screamed just above his head and continued on its course. Sgt. Kim smiled. Just try to run. Almost simultaneously three of Sgt. Kim's men had locked on and had good tones coming from their heat seekers, but nothing from the Stingers. That's odd, thought Sgt. Kim, why no radar? In a bloom of fire that made the entire valley look like daylight, the three missiles streaked into the night sky after their prey.

The tone in Colonel Hammer's helmet made his blood go cold. Shit! Immediately he released the flare to disorient the missiles and sprayed liquid nitrogen to cool the air behind him as his computer told him that the missiles had a heat signature and a high probable lock. Three inbound from his six o'clock. Time to dance, Sledge thought as he pushed the throttle to afterburner and pulled into a climbing 6G turn.

Go ahead, try to run, Sgt. Kim thought as he watched the intruder pull into evasive maneuvers. One of the three missiles fell for the maneuver, but the other two flew right past the flares and continued to their quest. The pilot continued to weave and dodge, but the two missiles found their mark in the hot engine of the F-22. With as far as stealth technology had come, the one problem that couldn't quite be solved was engine heat.

The impact came within seconds and Colonel Donald Hammer, husband and father, watched as his cockpit disintegrated before his eyes. In a second his whole world was flying around him at disorienting angles. The 6G's that he was pulling at the time of impact pressed him against his seat. Sledge could see the golden ejection handle in his mind's eye, just below the seat between his knees. Get that handle, Sledge. Pull the damned handle. With every ounce of strength that Sledge had, he reached for the handle and pulled.

At once he was rocketed from the twisted, disintegrating, burning metal that used to be his airplane and thrust even higher into the night sky. If nothing else the last evasive maneuver had gained him precious altitude. How much Sledge didn't know.

The gyros of the ACES II ejection seat activated and stabilized his attitude. Disoriented and confused, Sledge opened his eyes to see the earth rising towards him at a frightening pace. Still attached to the ejection seat, Sledge thought, either I'm above 14,000 feet or the damn thing is malfunctioning. There was no way to tell if the seat, or even chute for that matter, had been damaged in the explosion. He was actually surprised when the canopy popped off on cue, figuring that it had probably been twisted or misaligned in the fireball that used to be his plane. Almost in answer to his question, the seat separated and the chute deployed into the night sky above.

Must be at 14,000 feet. Sledge shook the cobwebs from his oxygen deprived, now aching head and started going through the routine of what he had been taught over and over again at the survival school at Fairchild AFB. Canopy, visor, mask, life preserver, survival kit, four-line release. Sledge began reciting the equipment check like it was some sort of a mantra. Canopy, visor, mask, life preserver, survival kit, four-line release...Canopy, visor, mask, etc. Ok Sledge, let's get to work. The voice inside his head was his own, and yet slightly detached. The strictly professional voice that comes from the years of training. The side that takes over when the rest of the world is going to hell in a hand basket.

Sledge looked up and checked his canopy. There, above him against the night sky, was the most beautiful piece of multicolored fabric in the world. Definitely owe life support a beer for this one. Sledge thought as he reached to his face, and for the first time realized that the ejection had ripped the visor and mask away from the helmet, cutting him slightly in the process. If that's the worst you get from this Sledge, you're a lucky man. As for the life preserver, it only activated upon contact with water, and since there was no water to be seen, Sledge just skipped that check and went to the next, survival seat. Probably the most important piece of luggage carried, it contained much of the essential survival gear Sledge would need to get out of this alive. Sledge glanced down and followed the twenty-five foot cord that acted as an umbilical cord to the vinyl rucksack, hit-and-run kit, and one-man rubber life raft below. All appeared to be in order.

Sledge then pulled the four-line release which activated the chute's steering controls by letting air billow out through designed holes in the canopy. Everything was in order. Thank you God, at least I've got that going for me. The one extra step in the routine, that wasn't taught in any of the survival schools, was to activate a special search and rescue beacon.

Normally this would be done on the Guard or Alpha channels, but this was a classified mission. The one thing that he had going for him in this theater of operations was that he was the only American anywhere in the area. Sledge reached inside his survival vest and brought out his emergency transmitter which was tethered to his vest, punched in the appropriate four digit code, and pressed the button which sent an encrypted message directly to one of the NSA's satellites through a series of relays. The message would then be repeated by one of the orbiting satellites continuously until a technician answered the call. The message relayed the last altitude and GPS location of Sledge and its activation was a confirmation that he was still alive. Being broadcast by the orbiting satellite, encrypted, and on various channels, and the fact that Sledge's actual transmission only lasted for thirty seconds, reduced considerably his detection by enemy forces.

Sledge focused his eyes on the ground below. He could see the tiny dots of light that he assumed were the flashlights of the people that would soon be searching for him, but for now they were busy heading towards the burning wreckage of the American aircraft. "Cindy" was now in pieces, scattered across the valley from one end to the other. Fuck you and your golden BB. In contrast to the first half of the ejection, this part was painfully slow. It felt as if time had stopped as he floated above a thousand searching eyes.

It wasn't until Sgt. Kim and his men had reached the main part of the wreckage that they discovered that the aircraft was American and the pilot had been able to eject. They had assumed that he was just one of the many falling pieces of fire, and now they realized that he was probably alive and on their land. Wow, what a trophy, thought Kim, if my team were able to produce the pilot... Definitely a promotion, maybe to officer. "Fall in." Sgt. Kim yelled and at once his team fell into ranks in front of their leader.

Twenty-five year old Sergeant Kim had joined the Army because in his mind, it was better than toiling for the State as a farmer, breaking his back day in and day out for meager wages. At least in the Army, he only broke his back part of the time, the rest of the time like now, he was the boss, and had others break their backs. If I can give my government the pilot, to show the world that America is not as strong and powerful as they thought, I would definitely deserve a promotion. Sgt. Kim began his briefing. "There is an American pilot somewhere in the area. We will fan out and do a grid search until we bring the intruder to justice. He is to be taken alive if possible, however, if necessary, you may shoot to kill. But again, try to take him alive. If taken alive, you all will get a seven day pass in addition to the two day pass already promised. Dismissed."

Colonel Hammer watched as what, in the dark, he assumed were trees approached from below. Sledge looked up at the night sky and cursed the calmness. If it had been even a little windy he would have traveled much farther away from the actual crash site. He reminded himself that there was good news. At least he was a couple hundred yards away from the clearing, and wouldn't be so easy to see land. The bad news, however, was that this was a heavily wooded area, and Sledge couldn't remember any instructor at jump school telling him to aim for trees.

Sledge brought his feet tightly together and slightly bent his knees as his feet grazed the soft branches of the tree tops. The trees loomed up from below as branches started to attack his legs and chest. Sledge put his hands in front of his face to protect his eyes from the contact, and at once the falling stopped as his chute tangled in one of the high limbs.

Great, thought Sledge, I'm going to be swinging here like a damned piñata. The chute had caught the highest, most unlikely branch, and as Sledge looked up to assess the situation, it broke. Colonel Hammer dropped like a rock through the remaining tree branches to the ground below. The forest floor was rocky and rough and as Colonel Hammer hit and tried to absorb some of the shock, a crack echoed through his body. As soon as he was free from the harness, he grabbed his hit-and-run kit and survival pack and headed deeper into the forest, barely noticing the pain shooting through his right ankle.

Okay the first thing they taught us at Fairchild, Sledge thought, focus and find cover, don't panic, just do. Colonel Hammer headed into the forest, stopping every couple of yards to listen and see if anyone was approaching. There was nothing except the sound of his own breathing. Thank God for small favors, Sledge thought. It was a slow and tedious process, and for the first time Sledge noticed the pain in his right ankle. Fuckin' A! Well Sledge, looks like we're going to have to find cover instead of run. Have to take a seat and wait for the cavalry.

Sgt. Kim and his men had, fortunately for Colonel Hammer, began their search on the top side of the clearing, thinking correctly that the light breeze would push him that direction. But they forgot to take into account the fact that the ejection seat of the F-22 was rocket assisted to project the pilot to a safe altitude, and at the time of ejection Colonel Hammer had actually cleared the meadow and was two miles to the south. The wind did bring him back towards the clearing, but he was currently a three quarters of a mile away from their search. Sgt. Kim thought for a moment about calling for reinforcements, and then decided that first he and his team would do the search. If they didn't find anything in the first hour he would make the call. If, however, they found something, they would be the heroes, and he would have his promotion.

The best cover Colonel Hammer could find was a huge bush, under an awning of pine trees. He crawled into the center of the bush and burrowed in like a wild animal. With his knife he dug out a shallow ditch, being careful as he was taught, not to disturb the appearance of the natural flow of nature. It was fine at night, for the only thing that the human eye picked up was movement, but during the day the eye would pick up anything that didn't fit with the natural landscape. And Sledge knew by daylight this area would be crawling with unfriendlies that wouldn't be the one's that had trained him at Fairchild. These, Sledge knew, would be out for his blood, and hopefully would follow the diversion he had set up to lead the hostiles in the wrong direction. He knew that it wouldn't do much, but any time gained was a positive. Sledge took out his camouflage stick and applied the green and loam paint to his face, neck and ears, tightened the lacing on his boot to support his injured ankle, and hunkered down as far as he could in the bush and waited.

By now those that were expecting him would know of his situation. All he had to do would be to play hide-and-seek long enough to stay alive. Sledge opened his survival kit and removed one of the small containers of water and quickly drank. Remember what they told you. Conserve water by limiting your movement. Don't get dehydrated. A dehydrated mind doesn't work. And stay still.

9 CRISIS

Notification of Colonel Hammer's situation came into the communication center of the Pentagon at 16:30 hours Eastern Standard time, during the afternoon meeting of the Joint Chiefs of Staff. The Sergeant that took the message, entered the meeting silently and proceeded directly to Air Force Chief. General Mitchell bit his lower lip and looked out the window at the inner courtyard of the five sided building, as the Sergeant whispered the news into his ear. "Any beacon?" General Mitchell asked automatically.

"Yes sir, the NSA says that they have a coded distress confirmation from Blue Steel's unit, and is actively scanning the area. Due to the radio traffic in the last hour they believe the North Koreans already have a search team in the area."

"Thank you Sergeant, keep me posted if any new developments occur."

The General turned back to face the other members of the Joint Chiefs of Staff, and cleared his throat. "As you all know, by order of the President, I have been running a classified operation trying to gather intel over North Korea. That operation, Operation Blue Steel has been intercepted, and we believe has been shot down over North Korea. We have an authenticated message transmitting his last GPS coordinates, so we know he's alive. We don't know the condition of the camera film and even if we did, it's now either lying in the mud of North Korea or melted and burned. So, it doesn't look like we are going to get that film of the facility until the boys at the NSA can re-program one of their satellite assets." The mood of the room, which had been sunny, turned dark.

"What do we tell the boss?" asked the Chief of the Army "Sorry, but your going to have to wait on that information you wanted."

"I think we've got bigger problems than him not having the intelligence to negotiate," answered Admiral McCullen, Chairman of the Joint Chiefs of Staff and Chief of the Navy. "He can bluff the North Koreans about their bombs, we KNOW they have the nuclear capability. But what if they get to the pilot first? Parade him in front of the news, do we realize what THAT would do to the summit. I'd be better off just turning in my resignation now."

"Well then let's get him back, what assets do we have available?" asked the Chief of the Army.

"Good question," answered Admiral McCullen. "Everybody's being watched so closely right now, we won't be able to lift a finger without bells and whistles going off all over North Korea. They know we'll be coming after him. Hell, it's what they want. If we go in with a SEAL team with guns blazing it will be all over their news. Hell, they probably have people watching SEAL teams One through Three as we speak. God Damn! the old man is really going to have our asses in a sling!"

"We have an option, Gentlemen." General Mitchell stated as he rose and walked to the window, pausing a moment to let the severity of the situation sink in. This was a huge decision. If the team was successful, he would secure more funding from the "special" budget next year, however, if they failed more American lives would be in jeopardy, and the Air Force would again look like the non-military branch of the service that was so unjustly put upon them by the other branches. It's all or nothing, thought General Mitchell.

"The option, gentlemen, is this. The Air Force has a team headed by Colonel Russell Mulgrave, that has been stationed out in the Nevada desert. They are trained specifically for a job like this. Pilot extraction. They are completely classified, operating at a Majestic clearance level. They have the equipment, the training, and most importantly the ability to do this. My suggestion is that we activate them."

There was a silence in the room as each of the four men weighed the options and thought about the possibility of success for a mission of this magnitude. The clock ticked off seconds that felt like hours.

Admiral McCullen was the first to speak. "This, of course, would have to be run by the President."

"Of course," answered General Mitchell.

"Very well," answered the Admiral, "since it's your idea, you get to be the lucky one to present it to the boss and I suggest you get over there right away. Gentlemen, it looks like we have a busy afternoon ahead of us, so if there's nothing more... everybody will give General Mitchell and his team all the resources at their disposal, let's get to work. Oh and Paul... Good luck."

"Thank you sir."

With that, the meeting was adjourned and General Mitchell walked down the hall to his office, closed the door, sat down, picked up the secure phone and called a certain secret base in Nevada. "Russ, it's Paul. I hope your boys are ready to go hot?"

The voice on the other end was an equal mixture, both confident and anxious at the same time. "Of course General. We're definitely ready."

"Good. I'll courier the mission specifics to Nellis, call your team and have them ready by tonight. I'll call with the go from the President when I get it. This is it Russ, this is real." General Paul Mitchell put down the phone, sat back in his chair, took a deep breath and remembered the time he was shot down. This time it was his friend.

10 FEAR

Sgt. Kim looked at his watch. Thirty more minutes to find the downed American pilot, or call for help. Kim looked around at his men searching the north end of the clearing, and then to the downed F-22. As he looked at the wreckage he pondered the ejection. If the plane landed there, and the pilot had time to eject, then wouldn't he have been farther out when he started his decent? He again looked at the clearing and his men searching the edges of the forest. Damn! I've wasted thirty valuable minutes. Sgt. Kim raised his whistle to his lips and blew three short times. His men stopped their search and formed a circle around their leader.

"I have decided to vary the search and now move to the south end of the meadow. Start your search at the edge of the forest and work inwards. Dismissed." Maybe there's still time, thought Kim. Maybe there's still time.

The whistle was the first sound other than those of the forest that Colonel Hammer had heard and it sent shivers down his spine. He had realized that people were going to be looking for him, but to hear the whistle confirmed that now they were. Well, thought Sledge, let the games begin. He felt like a fox hearing the bugle call to release the dogs. All he could do was burrow into his bush and hide. Sledge made a quick check to make sure there was nothing shiny or colorful visible, and looked out at the deception he had quickly made to lead any searchers away from his current location.

Sgt. Kim's team formed a straight line at the edge of the forest and began their search. Slowly, methodically, and meticulously the men searched the tree line looking for anything from the American jet, or anything that would lead them to the running American. Within minutes they had found the parachute and harness, which the American had tried to hide as he fled into the woods. Pretty good job, but not good enough, thought Sgt. Kim. He of course would have done it better. Concealed the parachute deeper into the woods and made it more obscured. He would have finished the job, not left it half done. Sgt. Kim called out to the other men in the area, "Concentrate on the area farther in the forest, the American entered here." Pointing to the tree that still held the remains of the American's harness.

The voices seemed to be right on top of him, but they were still a good twenty meters away. They had found his chute, but didn't seem to want to take the bait. Damn, thought Sledge, why don't you follow the trail? What are you waiting for? He could see one man who was issuing orders, and thought briefly about using his 9mm to take him out and make a run for it, going out in a blaze of Hollywood—induced American glory. He quickly dispelled the sweet fantasy as he remembered his training to wait for the right time, and until then, burrow in and hide. As he watched the North Koreans, the one that seemed to be the leader started issuing orders and the search team followed the trail Sledge had set. Sledge let out a sigh of relief and let his thoughts drift to his wife and daughter and prayed that he would again be able to hold them in his arms.

Slightly behind and directly next to him, Colonel Hammer heard the sharp crack of a stick breaking. Out of the corner of his eye, he could see the tip of an army boot and his heart stopped. Colonel Donald "Sledge" Hammer, father and Air Force pilot, held his breath, and for the first time in his life experienced raw fear.

One of Sgt. Kim's men noticed that the dirt by one of the bigger bushes had seemed to have been moved and decided to take a closer look. As he approached the bush to see if it was indeed natural, Sgt. Kim barked at the soldier to report back to the group immediately. Does he think that we're children? Why can't he just let us do our jobs? Thought the soldier as he headed towards Sgt. Kim. Colonel Hammer released the most important breath in his life.

Sgt. Kim looked at his watch. The hour was up. If he called for reinforcements now, he could claim that his radio hadn't worked and that he just now had been able to fix it that way avoiding disciplinary action. Damn, Sgt. Kim swore to himself, well, at least the reinforcements wouldn't be here for a little while. Maybe I could still get lucky. Or even with reinforcements, I could still be the one to find him, either way, I should still get a promotion. After all, it was my team that had shot down the American in the first place. Sgt. Kim walked to the middle of the clearing and called his superiors.

Thirty thousand miles away, at a barbecue in Las Vegas, four beepers went off almost simultaneously as SSgt. Mike Hecht came out of the back door and made the announcement to his team. "That was the Colonel on the phone, we have an alpha recall. Report time is immediately. There will be a plane waiting for us at Nellis to go up. Get your gear and meet there ASAP."

Mike Hecht hugged his wife and told her that he had to go to work, that it was some kind of exercise and that he would be home as soon as possible. Being a military wife, Sarah was used to the war games that were constantly played and knew that her husband would be home in a few days. "I'll get you a sandwich for your bag. I know how much you hate MRE's" Sarah kissed Mike on the cheek as she went to the kitchen to get the bread.

Mike gestured over to Chris, who was getting ready to leave. "Chris, can I talk to you for a second?"

Chris and Mike moved to the edge of the yard. "What's up?"

"I got a strange feeling about this. They have us going out of Nellis, and the Colonel said that he's sending down the Gulfstream for us."

"Don't read anything into it Mike, you've played war games before. You know how it is, they want you there real fast, and then you sit in a hangar that's supposed to be Korea, or Germany, or somewhere and eat MRE's all night." Chris smiled, slapping Mike on the shoulder. "Come on, let's go to Korea."

"Yeah, maybe. I just have a strange feeling about this one."

"That's just your stomach thinking about all those lovable

MRE's. I already have my gear in my car. You need a ride?"

"No. I'm going to say good-bye to Sarah and I gotta grab a few things. Save me a window seat."

"Gotcha." Chris asked if anyone else needed a ride, and then left to make the short drive to Nellis.

Sarah came back out of the kitchen and handed Mike his Kit Bag and the sandwich she had made for him. She always hated saying good-bye, especially for exercises. Sure, she was used to them, but they always made her wonder about the time that it wouldn't be an exercise, and what it would be like to say good-bye for that long. Mike kissed his wife and told her not to worry as he climbed into his jeep. "I'll call as soon as I can. I love you." Mike said as he kissed her one more time.

"I love you too. Be safe." Sarah said and watched her husband pull out of the car port and drive away.

11 DEPLOYMENT

The white Gulfstream was waiting on the tarmac of Nellis AFB as the four sergeants arrived at building 812. Within thirty-five minutes from the time of Colonel Mulgrave's phone call, Team One of Rescue Team Alpha was airborne and heading for Groom Lake. There had been alpha recalls before to assess their readiness, Colonel Mulgrave liked to be prepared, but this was the first time that the Gulfstream had flown out of Groom Lake during daylight. That's a new twist, thought Sgt. Ross as the team climbed to twenty-two thousand feet and banked north. I wonder what's going on?

Team One arrived at Groom Lake within an hour of the Colonel's call, and proceeded directly to the Nighthawk Nest, the nickname that they had given the hangar. Inside was Colonel Mulgrave, Team Two of the Nighthawks, and a doctor giving shots to the other members of the team. It was then that it hit Chris. *Holy shit. This is for real.*

The looks traded by the other members of the Nighthawks said the exact same thing. Each wondered where they were going and why.

"Always trust my gut." Mike whispered to Chris. "I guess we're going hot."

"What'd you expect, we live in the desert." Chris smiled. "It wasn't going to be cold forever."

Colonel Mulgrave spoke above the nervous chatter that had spread through out the room. "Gentleman. If I could have your attention please." The room quickly quieted as everyone listened to the Colonel. "If you haven't figured it out by now, we've been activated. We're going hot and hostile once we get authorization from the President. For right now I need you all to finish up getting your shots, get the equipment for a Code One operation, and report to the briefing room in one hour to receive mission specifics and assignments." With that the Colonel exited the hangar bay and went to his office.

As soon as he was gone the nervous energy once again enveloped the room. There was an electricity of excitement mixed with apprehension for the upcoming briefing. They were supposed to get gear for a Code One operation, which was a pilot extraction, possibly injured victum, with heavily armed and defended terrain. Most likely at night, but with the capability of daytime deployment. Detection by the enemy highly probable. Hostile engagement likely.

"Jesus. When we go hot, we go hot." Team Two leader, SSgt. David Miller said.

Nervous laughter filled the hangar bay as the rest of the team members traded looks of apprehension and excitement with each other.

After the shots were complete and the gear picked up, both teams took their seats in the briefing room as Colonel Mulgrave approached the podium. On each of the seats was a dark blue folder, sealed and stamped CLASSIFIED, MAJESTIC LEVEL CLEARANCE REQUIRED, OPERATION NIGHT ANGEL.

"Sergeant Hecht, would you please close and lock the door." Colonel Mulgrave waited until he had returned to his seat before proceeding. "Thank you. Well gentlemen, first of all, this briefing, of course, is classified. The blue folders that were on the seats when you entered contain the mission specifics, and we'll go over them in a minute, first I want to say something to you all. When Rescue Team Alpha was created, you were all told that you would be in support of the Nellis range. Now, I know some of you have speculated that Rescue Team Alpha was created for more than that. Most of you shouldn't be surprised at what you are about to hear. General Mitchell and I developed this team for the situation that has now occurred. This briefing is classified at the Majestic level.

"Our real mission has been from the conception, a quick response and pilot rescue team with the ability to go anywhere, anytime. It was what you all were trained for, what you all were selected for, and until today, you were to operate here on the test range unless or until something happened to change that. Well gentlemen, something has changed that, and earlier today I got the call from the Joint Chiefs of Staff asking if we were prepared to go active. So as of 16:00 hours this afternoon we are an active combat rescue unit." Colonel Mulgrave paused, and lifted one of the blue envelopes. "If you all will be so kind to open your folders, we can get started.

"The situation gentlemen is this. A little over two hours ago, one of our pilots, Colonel Donald Hammer, was shot down over North Korea. The details are sketchy but the NSA has an authenticated radio beacon, relaying the Colonel's last know GPS. We have also intercepted radio traffic from North Korea talking about the downed American jet. Judging from his flight profile, he probably ejected at an extremely low altitude at a high rate of speed, in a heavily wooded area, and is very possibly injured from that ejection.

"The political climate at the current time is in preparation for the upcoming summit, where it is believed our President is going to make some rather strong accusations concerning their nuclear capability. They would like nothing more than to get their hands on Colonel Hammer and parade him in front of the press to get sympathy for being bullied by the big bad American Air Force. Our job, gentlemen is to bring Colonel Hammer home alive to his little girl.

"If you will turn to the mission plan section of the folder, you will see the logistical plan that we will follow. Both teams, with the exception of Team One's pilots, will fly from Groom Lake to Kadena AFB in Japan, where you will stay until we get final go from the Pentagon. You will wear civilian clothes, to appear as businessmen and change into your gear in flight. You will then depart and intercept a civilian airline route that crosses twenty-two miles north of Colonel Hammer's estimated position, and perform a night HALO from forty-one thousand feet. If all goes well, and the weather is cooperating you will be able to reach Colonel Hammer with as little chute time as possible. A pair of Blackhawks from the 301st Special Operation Group in Japan will be on standby for the extraction. And a pair of F-16's from Kunsan will be on stand by to provide air support if necessary.

"We are now waiting for General Mitchell to brief the President and receive authorization, so I want you on the Gulfstream prepared to take off as soon as you have all your gear. Are there any questions?" Colonel Mulgrave looked at the room and smiled. "Good. I want to remind you, that you are the best. If I didn't think so, I wouldn't have risked my career by recommending this team to the General. All I know is that if I was in enemy territory, injured, cold, and hungry, after watching you all train and work for the last eight months, I would want you to be the team coming in for me.

"If you all have your gear, meet the pilots at the weather room in twenty minutes. There you'll get briefed on the weather conditions over North Korea and what you can expect in help from mother nature. If there's nothing else... Dismissed. Oh, and gentlemen, good luck."

As the team dispersed to make final adjustments, Colonel Mulgrave went to the secure phone in his office and called General Mitchell in Washington to inform him that the team was ready to go, sitting on the end of the runway, and awaiting clearance from the President.

General Mitchell hung up the secure phone and switched lines on his phone to call his assistant. "Jeff, have my driver meet me in the parking lot, I have to see the President as soon as possible." As he hung up the phone, General Mitchell picked up the blue folder of operation Night Angel and ran to the parking lot. Fortunately the traffic was light and within fifteen minutes General Mitchell's car pulled through the Secret Service checkpoint at the White House, and pulled up to the south entrance where he was escorted to the Oval Office's waiting room by the President's Chief of Staff.

This was the part that General Mitchell hated. Not making presentations or decisions, but waiting to go into the oval office. He had been here twice before to talk with the President and it always struck him as uncomfortable in the way that it looked like a museum. Maybe it was to remind the Presidents that occupied the office that no one ever really lived there, that they were only on an extended visit.

President David L. McKallister had been a "guest" in this office for the past two years, and in General Mitchell's mind, had done a pretty decent job. He had inherited, from his predecessor, a bunch of tangled knots in the way of domestic and foreign policy. Which, in fact, had been the main reason the public had put him in this office in the first place. He had won the Presidential election in a landslide, not so much because he was incredibly competent, which he was, but more that his predecessor was inept.

The only thing that his predecessor had wanted was to become President, and as a politician had sold his soul to the devil to accomplish that goal. His predecessor had of course won, and having no real vision or ideology to follow, he usually went with his whims. Throwing domestic and foreign policy into something that looked like a ship without a captain. David L. McKallister had jumped aboard that ship, grabbed control of the wheel, and had turned it on a course that the country was again proud of.

Of course the public wasn't aware of all the decisions that were made in this office. They didn't really want to know all of the details anyway. The public liked the vision that they held of their country. To them it was an honorable and innocent entity. What they didn't understand was that although it was a good thing to live by those ideals, the world didn't operate by those same rules, and to survive you sometimes had to do things you weren't exactly happy with. This was one of the reasons that Presidents aged so much, General Mitchell thought, because they were constantly having to worry about the outcomes of decisions they were never trained to make. It was a baptism of fire, and it made the office something that the General had no desire to obtain.

One of those decisions would have to be made today. Should the United States send a combat team in to another country to rescue a pilot that was on an intelligence gathering mission, risking the loss of lives on both sides and committing an act of war that could escalate an already tense situation. The answer of course, would be yes. It had to be. The decision had already been made earlier when he authorized the operation to get the intelligence in the first place.

There was also one of those unwritten American rules. You don't leave men who risk their lives stranded behind enemy lines. General Mitchell didn't quite know why we as Americans had made these rules or in what war it started, but it was one of those ideals that was handed down from one generation of warriors to another, from father to son. It was one of the reasons he was proud to be a part of the family of warriors.

The President's Chief of Staff came in and escorted General Mitchell into the Oval Office and closed the door. The office was smaller than it appeared in photographs, yet the power that emanated from the oak desk was enormous.

Painted a pale yellow with white trim, the office's federal architecture imposed an air of majestic power that carried out onto the view of the Rose Garden and beyond. President McKallister looked up from his desk and gestured to the seat in front. "Have a seat Paul. How's Jenny and the boy? Jeffrey figure out what he's doing when he graduates Georgetown yet?"

It had always amazed Paul how much detail the man behind the desk remembered about the people he dealt with. He didn't know if he had a briefing sheet, or if it was one of the many skills he had picked up over the years in politics. He assumed he had a sheet, but somehow he made the questions sound so innocent and real, you really didn't care.

"Jenny's fine, she's heading the officers' wives' club this year, and Jeffrey still hasn't decided but I think he's leaning towards law school, he loves to argue so it should suit him."

"Good. I'm glad to hear it. So now, what can I do for the Pentagon today, or should I say what are you going to do for me today. I understand we have a pilot down in Korea."

Blunt and to the point, as always, thought Paul. Actually it was one of the things that he found charming in the man. "Yes sir. Colonel Donald Hammer. Satellite recon and radio intercepts have confirmed that the North Koreans shot down his F-22 a little over an hour ago. They haven't mentioned the pilot yet, so there's a ninety percent probability that he's still evading. We did get an authenticated signal from the secure satellite showing his last GPS."

"He was the pilot on Operation Blue Steel?"

"Yes sir."

"And your plan is?" The President asked, knowing of course that the General wouldn't be here unless they had developed a plan over at the Pentagon.

"We have a team that is waiting on the end of the runway at Groom Lake, waiting for your authorization to proceed." The General handed the president the envelope containing Operation Night Angel. "They are a classified unit, highly trained in the preparation for a contingency like this. They will fly a civilian air route out of Japan, jump from an altitude of forty-one thousand feet and land within two miles of Colonel Hammer. Two Blackhawks from the 301st Special Operations Group will be on standby to make the extraction when the team is ready. The only outside people involved in the operation are the pilots from the 301st, and they're cleared, temporarily, for this mission."

A concerned look came across the face of the President "But we don't know for certain Colonel Hammer's status?"

"There hasn't been any indication from our intelligence assets, and there is always the possibility that they are following radio silence, but in my opinion, he's still evading sir."

The President stood and went to the window. The Rose Garden always provided a comforting solace, a certain peace that helped him focus thoughts in times of crisis. The President turned and faced General Mitchell. "Permission granted. Go bring Mr. Hammer back to his family."

"Yes sir. The team will be airborne within the hour."

"About this team General, congratulations on the foresight to develop them."

"Actually sir, the credit belongs to Colonel Russell Mulgrave. He approached me with the idea. The man's a real go-getter. Probably get my job one day. It's his baby I just made sure the pieces fit."

"Well, when this is all over, I would like to meet the man." The President smiled, "Oh and wish the team good luck for me, it looks like they're going to need it."

"Yes sir, I will." General Mitchell stood and prepared to exit. "As soon as the team's on the ground, I'll update you."

"Thank you Paul, I'll be expecting to hear from you. Give my regards to Jenny and Jeff, and again, good luck." President McKallister sat back down at the oak desk, closed the folder for Operation Night Angel, and prepared for his next meeting.

As soon as General Mitchell left the Oval Office he was escorted to the White House's Situation Room, where he was left to attend to the business that demanded his immediate attention. He picked up the secure phone from the oak conference table and called Colonel Mulgrave at Groom Lake. "Russ, it's Paul. You've got the green light, go get him back."

"Roger that General. The team will be airborne in ten minutes. They should be in Japan in fourteen hours."

"Good. Oh and Russ, the President wants to send the team his wishes and see you after this is all over."

"Lil' ol' me at the White House. Gee I don't know Paul, I might be busy that night."

The General smiled. "You'll put on your best clothes, clean up real nice, and pretend you like it. That's an order Russ."

"I'll give the team his wishes." Colonel Mulgrave paused for a moment. "Oh and General, thanks for going to bat for us. I've seen these boys train, they'll do the job."

"Don't thank me, just get Colonel Hammer back to his family and bring those boys home alive. Good-bye Russ.

Again, godspeed and good luck."

"Will do Sir, you have my word." Colonel Mulgrave hung up the phone in his office and called Nighthawk's Command Center, which was now being manned by the two pilots not on the mission. "Tell them they have a go, repeat they have a go. Also be advised," the Colonel was about to relay the President's message when he grabbed the hand-held from his desk and walked out into the sunlight and turned to the plane's frequency. "Big Bird this is Grover, be advised, the President sends his personal wishes with you. Bring our man home. Good luck. Contact Home Base when you get to Japan. Grover out."

"Copy that Colonel, permission to proceed. Contact when we arrive at staging area. Big Bird out."

The white Gulfstream at the end of the runway applied full throttle and starting rolling down the runway. Within seconds the plane's wheels lifted away from the safety of Groom Lake as Colonel Mulgrave stood in the afternoon sun and watched the plane disappear into the crystal blue sky.

12 HIDE AND SEEK

The sound of a distant helicopter filled the night air as Colonel Hammer strained his eyes to see what was going on. On the edge of the forest stood a group of shadows that were North Korean soldiers watching the lights of the helicopter as it came down into the valley. Since none of the soldiers were showing any signs of excitement Colonel Hammer figured that the chopper was expected, and was probably transporting more soldiers to help search the area. This is going to get very interesting, thought Sledge as he took the break in the search to adjust his body, and take a quick glance at his watch, 04:30, damn! Only ninety minutes until sunrise.

Lying completely still was starting to take a toll on his body. Cramps started attacking his back and legs, and something was crawling on his skin but he couldn't take the luxury to find out what it was. The not knowing was the hardest part. Sledge dismissed the thoughts from his mind, and tried to concentrate on relaxing his cramped muscles while he kept his attention on what was happening at the edge of the clearing.

Colonel Hammer could tell by the wind blowing through the trees and the way that the soldiers ducked their heads, that the helicopter was now in the process of landing in the clearing. In a minute the wind was gone and the sound of the helicopter faded into the quiet of the Korean night, and Colonel Hammer wondered whether the chopper would return carrying even more troops. As Colonel Hammer squinted he could see the group at the edge of the clearing come to attention and salute the approaching group.

Sledge could tell by the way that the group moved that they were not officers, but enlisted men, workers. Which meant because of the previous salute, that there was an officer in the group. Well, finally came out to take charge huh, thought Sledge, probably looking for a promotion.

Captain Rhee Ho-Shim, was twenty-six years old, and a promotion was the last thing on his mind. Raised by his father after his mother had died, Captain Rhee had been taught at a very early age the communist idealism and beliefs of his father. His father was a hero of the Korean war, and was injured fighting for those principles. Principles that he taught young Rhee to believe in. His father schooled him in all of the basic disciplines and when Rhee reached the age of eighteen, enrolled him in the University of Southern California and sent him off to America to study. The money, Rhee knew, came from his father who had saved all of his pension from the Army, forgoing meals when he could, and making due with what he already had so that Rhee could go to America to learn the things that his country needed to survive, and Rhee vowed not to let him down.

Rhee learned many new things in America, one of the most important lessons, not coming from school, but from the country itself. America was supposed to be a place for freedom, but everywhere Rhee turned, he saw less and less freedom, and more and more oppression. Teens were running lawless in the streets, basically untouched by the police. Minorities were mistreated and held below the poverty line, and the government taxed the people more and more. Living in America had taught Rhee that Communism was the only free society. The only kind of civilization that allowed a society to become its most productive, its most useful self. True freedom. After USC Rhee returned to his homeland and decided that the best ways to use his new talents would be in the Army, protecting the ideals, beliefs, and people that made Korea so strong.

He was at once made an officer and sent to very demanding training schools designed to make him more efficient than he already was. Better, braver, smarter. He had graduated at the top in his class and was assigned to an infantry unit, where he quickly won the support and respect of his fellow officers, including those who outranked him, and had advanced to the rank of Captain faster than anyone in the infantry, ever.

And now this. America, the country that he despised the most had once again sent one of their jets to spy on his people. When will they stop? When will they leave us in peace to grow strong? What are they afraid of? Captain Rhee and the squad of reinforcements joined the group at the edge of the clearing.

"Where is Sergeant Kim?" Captain Rhee asked as he returned the soldier's salute.

As the soldier started to reply Sergeant Kim exited the forest, approached Captain Rhee and saluted. "I am Sergeant

Kim. It was my unit that shot down the American intruder, and we have started a search of the area."

"I am aware of who shot down the jet Sergeant; there is no need for you to brief me on details that, right now, I neither need, or care to know. Do I make myself clear?"

"Yes sir." replied Sgt. Kim.

"What I do need to know is how much of this area has been searched. How much time the pilot had until you started the search." Captain Rhee smiled. "And why you waited so long before calling in for reinforcements." Sergeant Kim declared that they had started the search immediately, that he had tried to call for reinforcements but for some unknown reason the radio had trouble transmitting, and then showed the Captain on the map, the sectors that they had already searched.

Colonel Hammer overheard the voices and assumed that the officer was being briefed on the night's activities. Dawn had started turning the sky a little bit lighter color of blue. Only one star remained visible. Venus, or Jupiter, Sledge could never remember which. As he evaluated his situation, Sledge considered moving to another location that had already been thoroughly searched, but decided that the risk was far greater than the benefits. Sledge's mind started to drift to thoughts of his little girl. Memories of her playing on the swing, running for the ice cream truck, and other idyllic memories that may or may not have happened the way that they appeared in his mind. He knew that he couldn't have the luxury of these daydreams often, yet he also knew that they gave him the will to survive. The only thing that mattered to Sledge at this moment was to have his little girl in his arms again.

Captain Rhee stood in the clearing looking towards the woods where they had earlier found the parachute and harness. Why did you leave the parachute and harness so visible? Were you trying to lead us away or just careless? You're training has to be better than that American, so maybe you're just trying to be clever. Captain Rhee called Sergeant Kim over to instruct where to search. Rhee didn't like Sergeant Kim. Dislike wasn't a strong enough word, and Rhee didn't know if he could actually hate another countrymen, but if he could, this would be the one. In Rhee's eyes Sergeant Kim was everything that was wrong with his society. Greedy and self-serving, never thinking of the greater good, just about what they would get out of it. Captain Rhee knew that earlier the radio had been working properly, and probably now still was, and that the Sergeant just wanted to be a hero and find the pilot himself. But he never gave a second thought to the fact that the longer he waited to call in reinforcements, the more likely it was for the American to get away and that course would be worse for the country. He would have to deal with that later, thought Captain Rhee, right now I need his manpower to find the American. I just hope he doesn't do anything else foolish.

"I want you and your men to continue their search deeper into the woods, starting from the area that you found the parachute, and place two men to secure the crash site. I will take a squad and head to the south to see if there is a trail. The American is probably still in the area so be quiet. It's harder to hide from something that you don't know the exact location of."

Sergeant Kim saluted. "Yes sir." The answer coming out just a little more sarcastic than he intended.

Smartass, thought Captain Rhee. It was in the inflection of the way he said it, nothing that the Captain could hold against him, but enough to show his displeasure. Captain Rhee smiled. Insolent fool, just wait until this is over.

"And give your men a five minute break every thirty minutes. Dismissed Sergeant."

Captain Rhee looked at the shades of blue above his head and realized that the sun would rise in a couple of hours. Well there's a break for us. It was much, much harder to stay concealed during the day. The sunlight highlighted even the tiniest of mistakes.

Colonel Hammer looked up, saw the same sky, and cursed, knowing that there would be very little time left where he had the advantage.

Sergeant Kim and his team passed within ten feet of Colonel Hammer's position as they proceeded to the spot where they had found the parachute. Little did they know how close they were and Sledge held his breath as he wondered what they would do next. What was their plan? Who was their new leader and did they want to capture him alive? To Sledge's delight the team continued deeper into the woods, farther away from his position. The other team Sledge noticed, had headed slightly behind his position before they left his field of vision. Although Sledge couldn't see them, the sounds of the team seemed to also be heading deeper into the forest.

Sledge again looked at the sky and decided that if he was going to move, he would have to do it now, before the sky became too bright. The positive thing was that the time right before dawn, was one of the most difficult times for vision. Sledge did another quick look at the area and noticed that the two men standing at the crash sight were smoking cigarettes. Great, thought Sledge, Thank God for small favors. Night vision was a very fragile thing, and something as little as a lit cigarette could ruin it for at least twenty minutes.

Sledge took a deep breath, and slowly crawled out from under the bush. Staying very still and silent for a minute while he listened to the sounds of the forest, Sledge could hear nothing in his area. He could hear the faint sounds of the team that had passed by him deeper in the woods, but other than that, there was almost an eerie silence.

The first priority was to find a source of water, and since the Koreans were deeper in the forest, he would have to hope that on the edge of the clearing somewhere was a spring that he could get to. Besides it would give him an opportunity to scout the clearing for his rescue. The major problem with being on a classified mission and being shot down was that there were no other friendly aircraft flying overhead that you could signal with the emergency radio and beacon. Besides, if you used the beacon, something that the Korean's would be scanning for, you might as well just walk out into the clearing and surrender. Sledge knew that by now the Pentagon had satellite images of the F-22 wreckage, had received his encrypted message, and had enough information to determine that he was alive, probably not yet caught, and was waiting for help. The question in Sledge's mind was would they send a team this close to the summit. Of course they would, thought Sledge. They had to. All he would have to do is stay out of enemy hands and wait.

The clearing was a perfect place for an extraction. Remembering the terrain from his approach into the valley, Sledge knew that this was the only clearing in the forest for miles, and the most likely spot for a helicopter to land.

Sledge slowly approached the edge of the clearing and peered out into the darkness. The entire field was still dark in the early dawn, save for the two red glowing dots that came from the soldiers' faces. The light was just enough to give a definition to their faces and Sledge noticed that they were only boys, barely out of their teens. But wasn't that the way it always was, thought Sledge, even in his own military, the new faces coming in each month seemed to look younger and younger. Maybe I'm just getting older and older. Sledge knew that the young age of the soldiers was to their disadvantage since they wouldn't be quite as disciplined as the older soldiers, and from the smoking, it was evident. Probably have only played war games. Never been to the front. If they had spent any time on the DMZ they would have known never to smoke at night, especially on the DMZ where a cigarette glow provided the perfect aiming point for a sniper on the other side.

Colonel Hammer very slowly and quietly started exploring his immediate area for any clues that could tell him the whereabouts of water. The ground was dry, save for the moisture of the morning dew that had formed through the night, and the carpet of pine needles insulated the little noise that Sledge made.

Attending Flight Crew Escape and Evasion training at Fairchild AFB, Sledge had thought that the instructors had taken things just a little too seriously. Sure, what they had taught was important, but they were American Fighter Pilots, and most had seen the training as just another break from the day to day routine of their own bases.

Now, however, in the mountains of North Korea, Sledge was more than thankful for those weeks of hell in the forests of Washington. It had become so real, including a POW camp, that at the end of the training, when they lowered the Soviet flag and raised the American flag tears had come to his eyes. The training had been so real that Sledge had begun to think that the training was reality and that his previous life was just a part of his imagination. Several trainees had to be removed from the program due to stress and the emotional havoc that it produced. There were actually two separate, but equally important parts of the school operating at Fairchild. Part one of the school was to teach you the tactics and survival skills that you would need to save yourself if you were ever shot down. Where to find edible food, how long you could last without food, how to find shelter and water, the two things that if you didn't find immediately, you would die. All the book stuff.

Part two of the school was more intense. It was where you tested the new skills that you learned. Set up as a POW camp, the instructors drop you in the middle of the forest with your parachute and gear that you would have if you had just ejected, and told you to go. From there you were to evade capture as long as possible, but if you were captured you were taken to the mock POW camp where you were expected to act as if it was a real camp.

People formed into groups, with the most senior taking command. The goal was to escape. And to allow yourself to enter the mental state required to survive. The Pentagon knew that the only way to do that was make the camp so real, so tangible, that your other reality faded into the dark corners of your mind. By practicing a kind of psychological warfare on the students, the camp became their reality.

There were no failures at the camp, for it was to give you something to hold onto if, indeed, you ever were shot down. You could take solace in the fact that you had been through this before and you would get through it again. At the time Sledge had thought it was all just a little too much, putting people in such a mental state, just for training purposes, but now, in the early morning behind enemy lines, with an injured ankle, he was grateful. Extremely grateful.

The pain in Sledge's ankle had increased with the swelling, and was now to the point where he could take only a few steps without stopping for a moment to rest. In some ways this was a blessing, for it forced him to stop every few feet and listen to his surroundings, something that was taught in Fairchild, but very hard to do with adrenaline flowing through your body. Everything was now at a heightened sense of awareness for Sledge. It felt as if he could see more clearly, hear more clearly, and smell more things in the environment. The heightened concentration also made it feel like he could sense every pore, every muscle in his body.

He moved slowly along the perimeter of the forest, keeping the red glow of the soldiers cigarettes in view, but staying out of their line of sight. In the distance he could hear the two teams of Koreans as they continued their search for him. Sledge didn't know if they sounded so close because they were or if it was because of his heightened senses and the fact that sounds travel farther at night. He hoped it was the later, because if they were that close he would have to find another hiding area quick.

For a moment Sledge thought he could see the hint of movement in the forest and froze. A lone soldier came running out of the forest and approached the other two soldiers at the crash site. Sledge couldn't see what was happening but could hear words being exchanged between the soldiers, and then one of the other soldiers entered the forest where the first one had exited, leaving again two at the crash site.

A little too busy for me, thought Sledge as he traversed the fifty feet back to the bush which had become his home. The entire trip had lasted twenty minutes, yet in Sledge's mind it felt like two hours. He crawled back into the base of the bush and made his surroundings again look as natural as possible. Within ten minutes the two teams returned to the crash site and Sledge watched as the sky turned faint colors of orange as he reapplied the camouflage face paint to his ears and neck and prepared for the inevitable daylight, while the soldiers took a break from the search and began to eat breakfast.

Captain Rhee looked up at the colors changing in the morning sky and watched as dawn slowly made its way across the Korean countryside. This was the time that he enjoyed the most. Dawn. Most people hated dawn. It meant the beginning of another day of toil. Captain Rhee, however, relished it. To him it meant a new day, another chance to do well. Another day to serve his country. This part of the Korean peninsula was only remotely inhabited and Rhee watched as the fingers of light started stretching their way across the green trees and life within them. The nocturnal birds had long since entered their nests for rest, and the birds of day took their place in the flow of the valley. The westerners could never understand his people, thought Rhee, because they didn't understand the beauty in their homeland. The majestic hills, the flowing waters, and even the harsh conditions were all beautiful to Rhee. In fact it was partly the harsh conditions that made the country what it was. Having to live under these circumstances made only the strong stay. Only those who loved their life here remained. The rest, like driftwood in the ocean, went away. Rhee smiled at his country and the beauty it was sharing with him as the sun crested the eastern mountain top and spilled over into the valley.

General Mitchell opened the envelope on his desk and took out the thermal images from the NSA. Technology was amazing, thought Paul. Here it was the middle of the night in Korea, and darkness couldn't even hide you from other's orbiting eyes. The images on Paul's desk showed the clearing in a thermal pattern. Not like an ordinary picture, thermal images were the signatures left by objects that contained heat. At the edge of the clearing was what appeared to be the wreckage of the F-22, still showing signs of heat, although not a lot. By the wreckage were the very high signatures of two people, probably North Koreans guarding the crash site, thought Paul. Then off to the north were two groups, one consisting of thirteen men, the other eleven. Probably search teams. And then, at the edge of the clearing, just inside the tree line, was a lone signature, in the general area of the crash, but away from the other figures. A smile came across General Mitchell's face. Well Colonel Hammer, I hope getting you out is as easy as finding you. General Mitchell picked up the phone and dialed Colonel Mulgrave at Groom Lake.

"Russ, it's Paul again, "

"Yes sir, what's up."

"We've located the Colonel. I'm sending intel for the team across the scrambled command channel."

"I understand." answered Colonel Mulgrave, "I'll be waiting in ops."

"Good, call to confirm when you get it." General Mitchell hung up the phone and looked at the photo on his desk. "Congratulations Colonel Hammer, you just increased your chances." Paul took a sip of coffee and called Sergeant Davis to get the picture sent electronically to a specific secure phone number and to have a copy couriered to the Oval Office.

13 LOGISTICS

The flight from Groom Lake was quiet. The eight members of the Nighthawks sat alone with their fears and apprehension for the first leg of their journey. One or two checked over their gear, but the rest, like Chris, stared out the window. Chris, intellectually, agreed with the reason for this mission. Emotionally, however, well, the flight was too long and the first dose of adrenaline had already worn off leaving Chris anxious.

Being that the age of all the Nighthawks was below thirty, this was the first combat any of them had seen. Chris had come close, during Grenada, but was just out of training and was technically en route to his new base when the recall had come. If the date on his orders had been one day sooner, Chris would have gone, but it wasn't, so he didn't. But now this. What was it MSgt. Parker had said? Putting yourself in harm's way, on purpose, was slightly crazy. So here they were, eight technically sane individuals, about to jump out of a perfectly good airplane, on purpose, into hostile territory where people wanted to shoot you, and they would all do so willingly. Someone should redefine the word sane, Chris thought as he stared out at the cloud formations passing beneath them. Chris shook the thought from his head and took out the envelope that contained the mission specifics. Inside was a picture and report on Colonel Hammer, who Chris remembered, had a wife and daughter. A family. Chris stared at the picture and wondered what it would be like to lose your father and not being able to know the reason, just that his plane crashed. Not knowing the real reason, that your father had died in the service of his country. Died doing a service asked of him for reasons unknown except to the people who did the asking, to put himself in harm's way for the protection of his country. And because of his oath, because of his honor, and because of the love he felt for his country, went into harm's way unquestioningly. I won't let that happen sir. If you're alive, you're coming out alive, back to your little girl. Chris put the picture back in the folder, closed his eyes, and tried to nap.

The first stop on the Nighthawk's flight was Hickam AFB in Hawaii where the team had to make a few civilian purchases. Their cover was as businessmen on a trip from the U.S. to Japan and then onto China. And since there was going to be time to kill in Japan while they waited for the night, now was the time to shop. It was nothing that some cash and a little help from a department store couldn't fix. In no time at all, the eight members of Rescue Team Alpha looked less like military personnel and more like the young executives of a twentieth century American corporation.

Each of the members had received a gold Corporate American Express card issued to NDB Incorporated. It was an inside joke to the members of the Nighthawks, who had found out that Colonel Mulgrave had established NDB Inc. as a money channel from the Pentagon. When the team members first had received their cards and asked what NDB stood for, Colonel Mulgrave turned and with the slightest smile answered None of your Damned Business. And so now the team members were executives for NDB Inc. on a business trip for reasons that were none of anyone's damned business.

After purchasing the items that they needed, the Nighthawks boarded their Gulfstream and continued to their original destination of Tokyo's Narita International Airport. While the flight was en route to Japan the team received a radio transmission from Colonel Mulgrave. Once the team had hotel rooms in Japan, they were to wait for a courier to provide them with new information, get some rest, and proceed at the earliest possible moment.

The Gulfstream landed in Tokyo and taxied to the corporate flight center which provided taxies and town cars to the local hotels. The members of the team were taken by taxi to the hotel at the edge of the airport. To say that the accommodations were plush was an understatement. Being on an unlimited expense account had its perks, Chris thought. The Nighthawks had been split two to a room, all on the 4th floor of the hotel, and began their wait for instructions. The wait didn't last long, not even enough time to nap, as the courier arrived and brought the package to Captain Foster who, because of his rank, was acting commander as well as lead pilot.

After calling the team together and reviewing the images, it was decided that the operation would begin at 23:00 hours. They would be over their jump site around zero-one hundred, and now had about five hours to get some rest. The clock ticked off minutes that seemed like hours as the members tried to keep their minds off of the upcoming mission. Some tried to find American shows on the TV, play cards, or just paced back and forth, anything to get their minds off of the "what if" scenarios that were running through their heads. The helicopters for the extraction part of the operation were already airborne from Kadena AFB in Japan, to Kunsan AFB in South Korea, where the response time would only be thirty minutes from the time of the Nighthawks call, and were ready to go on standby as soon as the team dropped into North Korea. It was the beginning of what would be a long night.

14 STALKED

During the daylight hours, Colonel Hammer hid in the bush as still and quiet as humanly possible, barely moving as parts of his anatomy fell asleep and became numb. Some of the cramps became almost unbearable. Roots, rocks, and branches constantly poked and stabbed his body as he contorted himself into strange positions to keep invisible. The boredom and anxiety were almost unendurable, and the pain in his ankle was a constant reminder of how vulnerable he was. All he could do by day was hope, pray, and wait.

In his pain he would try to take his mind off of the situation by imagining that he was home with his wife and little girl, that the sun he felt burning through his flight suit, scorching his neck, was the sun at the beach and that he was lying on a towel with his family around him. If he closed his eyes, he could almost hear the waves of the ocean, and the sound of the children's laughter as they played in the surf. Usually he could live in one of these fantasies for hours. Until his attention was distracted by the sound of approaching soldiers, or by another bug bite that was added to his already large collection, and his mind snapped back, kicking and screaming, to reality.

The soldiers were now in their own routine. Since they had already searched the area around Sledge twice, their focus now shifted deeper into the woods. They were content that the American pilot was no longer in the general area. This was both good and bad news to Sledge. Good because now they were a little more lax around the surrounding area and had relaxed their attitudes around the crash site. They weren't as vigilant and that allowed Sledge the small luxury of being able to move in very tiny amounts. Bad because now they were much more likely to discover him on one of their many trips to use nature's bathroom, which the Koreans had decided would be a bush not too far from his own.

It could have been worse, Sledge knew. They could have selected his bush. Because of this development, soldiers randomly just appeared in his area, and had already almost literally stepped on him in their treks in and out of the woods.

Tonight he would move carefully to search for water, food, and possibly a new location to hide, farther away from the action. Water would be the priority since it had been a hot sunny day and Sledge knew that the body could last thirty days without food, but only seven days without water. He had no idea how long it would be until he was rescued.

Captain Rhee placed the map on the hood of the vehicle and unrolled it. The search had gone well today, with five square miles covered, yet they were still unable to find the American pilot. Where are you American? Are you moving ahead of our search, or dug in hiding somewhere? Captain Rhee knew that time was running out for both parties. The summit would be in two days, and if he didn't produce the pilot by then a key political opportunity for his country would pass. He also knew that the Americans thought the same and would probably be sending a rescue team to extract the pilot. If there was one thing he learned about America while he was there, is that contrary to what his country thought because of Vietnam, they always tried to rescue their heroes, and they too would come for this one, dead or alive. Since his men hadn't picked up an emergency beacon or communication from the pilot, he assumed that the Americans hadn't either. That meant that they would probably start their search here at the crash site.

He had requested more reinforcements, knowing what would come, but was told that they were needed elsewhere during the summit as a show of force, and that the likelihood of an American rescue this close to the summit was small. The commanders in Pyongyang, just don't understand the Americans, thought Rhee. Now, looking around at the unit that he had with him he wondered if it would be enough. Yes, if the plan is sound, timed perfectly, and executed properly, these will be enough.

Now it was just a matter of coming up with the proper plan. Captain Rhee again looked at the map. If the Americans were to send a team, to come in undetected, they would probably follow the same strategy that they had before, by coming in from the south and staying below radar. It would probably be a small team of Marines or Special Forces in helicopters to secure the area and extract the pilot and that meant that they would be able to hear their approach. They still had some Stinger rockets left, and with the advanced warning they could set an ambush. Then we would really have something for the summit, thought Rhee and he smiled. Captain Rhee called Sgt. Kim on the radio and told him to return to the command post immediately for special instructions.

When Sgt. Kim arrived he was briefed on taking his team and sealing off the northern end of the valley, beginning at dusk, while Captain Rhee and his men would seal off the southern end. Also given to the men was the order and authorization to fire upon any unannounced helicopters. Until then, they were to continue searching the surrounding woods.

Colonel Hammer slowly took a look at his watch. It was now 17:00 hours and the sun would be going down in about two hours. Just two more hours until he could move a little more and release the pain in his joints. The stiffness that had accumulated was almost as bad as the pain in his ankle and Sledge winced as the focus shifted to his ankle. It was amazing how, with nothing to do, your senses would shift to a certain area just by thinking about it. He had now been on enemy territory, playing hide and seek for fifteen hours. Without food, water, or sleep, Sledge wondered how long it would be until his mind started playing tricks on him. He closed his eyes and again returned to the beach with his wife and daughter.

15 HOT ZONE

The Nighthawks took off from Narita International Airport at 23:00 hours and headed south-west towards the filed destination of Beijing, China. Departing dressed in business attire, the team now began preparing for battle. Each member shed the costume of corporate America and began the metamorphosis to fighting soldiers, applying camouflage paint to their hands and faces, dressing in black BDUs, and applying burlap strips to their weapons to help break up the visual outline.

Since this would be a night operation, and since the Nighthawks didn't want any uniform that could identify them as distinctly American, the team dressed in specially designed jet black BDUs. Created specifically for night operations, the BDUs were treated with chemicals that confused night observation and infrared devices. It didn't make you completely invisible, but distorted your image enough to allow you to blend in with the surrounding shadows. Chris wasn't exactly sure how it worked, and didn't believe they would until he had seen the demonstration. But they did, and that was all that really mattered. They had done everything that camouflage was supposed to do, basically breaking up the human form into a shape that was not immediately visible as a definite shape causing your mind to look elsewhere.

Chris looked around the plane and took a deep breath to calm his nerves. The tension was the same as it had been on the first night HALO over the Nevada Desert, the only difference was that this was for real and so everything was just a little more sharp, and the fear was a little more defined. Chris caught Mike looking at a picture of Sarah as he put his personal gear in the compartment below the seats. "It's going to be all right Mike. We go in, we get out, and we bring a father home to his little girl."

"I know," Mike smiled sadly, "I just wish I had said a proper good-bye. I thought it was an exercise. I thought that we'd be home in a day or two."

"We still will Mike. You can give her a proper hello instead," Chris paused. "Hell they don't even know we're coming. We'll be in and out before they even know we were there. Promise."

Mike started to check the sling on his weapon and the ammo in the magazine. "Maybe, but I still have that feeling in my stomach, and you know how I feel about that."

"I told you before, it's the MRE's." Chris began to check his own weapons.

Chris was the hostage sniper for Team One and because of that had special requirements. Normally he would just use one of the two JARs, just another rifle, made especially for the Secret Service that Colonel Mulgrave had managed to acquire. But he knew that there was little chance of Colonel Hammer being held hostage and so he had chosen to bring two weapons on this mission. The JAR for precise work and the H&K MP-5 because it was light and extremely accurate and fired a three round burst automatically. The extra weight would slow him a step or two but not enough to matter.

Chris brought his equipment over to where Mike was and sat next to him.

"Look Chris," Mike said as he glanced out at the stars passing above them. "If anything should happen to me, help Sarah with everything when you get back. We don't have any family and she's going to need help. Could you do that for me?"

"You know not to think like that. Besides, if anything happens to you, don't you think it will happen to me too?" Chris smiled. "Look, Mike, if it will make you feel better, I promise, but you gotta stop thinking like this man. Keep your edge." Chris slapped Mike on the shoulder and they smiled at each other.

Funny, Chris thought, we really are so different. Every member of the team had his own quirks and foibles. You wouldn't be able to find a more diverse group and it was that diversity that was their strength. Each excelled where another was weak, and Chris realized that he now knew what he had only thought in the hangar on that first day. In a heartbeat, he would give his life for any one of these men, and that they would do the same. They would be bonded now forever. Going into combat changed a man and they would be changed together.

The thought was shattered by the announcement from the copilot that they were ten minutes from the insertion point. The weather had smiled upon the Nighthawks as the winds were blowing in their favor, so that it would be no trouble to cover the twenty miles needed to make the crash site. It also meant that they could open their chutes lower and avoid the off chance that someone might see them floating in the night sky.

The two teams made last minute checks of their equipment and went over the operation plan one last time. The Nighthawks were to drop into the clearing about a mile away from the actual crash site, and using the tree line as cover, proceed to the crash site where they would separate into two teams. Team Two would secure the landing area and crash site recovering the film from the gun camera if possible. Team One would search the area for Colonel Hammer and provide medical treatment if necessary. When Team One had contact with Colonel Hammer they would call for the extraction helicopters who would be flying a holding pattern on station fifteen minutes out. The two teams would then reform along the tree line to await the helicopters' arrival. They were to engage the enemy only when necessary and avoid combat if possible.

When all of the team members were in their proper combat gear and had their oxygen turned on, the copilot put on his own mask, closed the door to the cockpit and signaled the pilot to depressurize the rear cabin. Once over the drop zone the copilot opened the rear door, and acted in the capacity of jump master, notifying when each of the members were clear and when to jump. Chris looked at his watch, adjusted his altimeter, closed his eyes, and said a quick prayer.

Chris stood at the edge of the door and again looked into the abyss. This time, it was different. With a reason and a mission, and the picture of a little girl in his head, jumping out of a perfectly good airplane was as easy and natural as falling out of bed.

When all the members of the Nighthawks were out, the copilot resealed the door and went back to the cockpit for the continuation of the flight. As soon as the teams were clear the pilot called Sesame Street on the radio and told Grover that the Muppets were on their way.

16 STAR LIGHT, STAR BRIGHT...

The night, so far, had been good to Sledge and he had been able to leave the shelter of his bush to search for food and water. The most peculiar thing about the night was the lack of a search team. At sundown, Sledge had watched as the team split into two different groups and moved to opposite sides of the valley. Each team had taken a supply of Stinger Missiles and Sledge was left to wonder if they knew something that he didn't. Maybe they're expecting a rescue attempt thought Sledge. Maybe they intercepted a radio transmission out of the south. Either way Sledge decided it would be wise to stay close to the area, just in case there was a rescue attempt. He also decided that it would be prudent to search for a source of water.

The two teams had dispersed to opposite ends of the valley over three hours ago, and Sledge started to enjoy his new freedom. The ankle still sent shooting bolts of pain through his body, but the ability to stand and lean against a tree for a while had relieved Sledge of the cramps. For Sledge the feeling was not unlike diving into an icy cold pool on a hot July day, or falling on the bed to sleep, after being awake for twenty-four hours. Hmmm, sleep. That would be nice, thought Sledge, to sleep in a nice, soft, warm bed, and have his hair caressed by his wife. Yeah, that would definitely be nice.

In the three hours since the teams had left the area, Sledge had worked his way across the clearing on his stomach. It took him a little over thirty minutes to reach the other side, but the time and risk were well spent as right inside the tree line was a small brook of fresh water. Careful not to make much noise, Sledge took the purification tablets and collapsible cup from his vest, mixed the solution with the water, and drank; being careful not to drink so much as he would get bloated, or sick if the water was heavily tainted. Just enough to keep him from dehydrating.

The brook also had a source of small, tender, edible ferns, from which Sledge made a survival salad, again, just enough to quiet his stomach, but not too much in case there was a heavy bacterium in the area. Better safe than sorry, thought Sledge, you can go a month without the food, don't risk it. Sledge looked around at the area and decided that it would be better to stay on this side of the clearing, since it was closer to water, and the soldiers had a habit of coming very close on the other side. Sledge looked around to make sure the soldiers weren't using this particular brook for their own uses, and found a group of bushes, that when the time came, would do nicely as a new home.

Sgt. Kim's team had reached the north end of the valley at sundown, just as Captain Rhee had ordered, but so far had seen or heard nothing, and his men were starting to get bored and tired. This is insane, thought Sgt. Kim, why are we out here wasting valuable time when we should be looking for the American pilot? They would never send a rescue team into North Korea this close to the summit. Why would they want to risk looking like fools? They know that there would be no way of succeeding. Sgt. Kim looked out over the dark Korean valley. No, they wouldn't send a rescue team, not so soon. Not into Korea. So maybe... I could still find the pilot with my team... and still come out of this with a promotion. Sgt. Kim decided to disobey a direct order and use his team to find the American pilot on his own.

On the other end of the valley Captain Rhee's men had set up a defensive line across the clearing, and as he looked out across the peaceful valley, the country of his people, Captain Rhee knew in his heart that he would down any aircraft that came to try and free the fallen intruder, and deny his country the justice it deserved. Since the Korean war, America had always tried to prove to his people, usually by force, that democracy was the only true way to freedom. That was just not so.

They had even conned the South into the idea. And as much as they espoused freedom, they were just as much against it as the countries that they tried to claim were the villains. Here was his own country, who couldn't, because of America's presence, expand and grow and reclaim and unite the two Koreas. Couldn't heal the wounds that so desperately needed to be healed so that his country could survive and be one again. And now this. They send in spies to scare his leaders to stop developing nuclear weapons. Why? Because it would also give North Korea the power that they needed to prove to their brothers in the South that democracy is not the only way? Well it was about time that they took my country seriously, thought Rhee, very seriously.

Sgt. Kim assembled his men in the northern part of the valley and told them that they had just received orders from Captain Rhee to resume searching for the American pilot. They spread out in to the forest, and once again began their desperate search, leaving the northern most edge of the clearing unprotected.

Since the soldiers were away from his part of the valley, Colonel Hammer had time to dig out an area of the bush that would contour to his body, without the sticks, rocks and thorns of the old one, and again make it look as natural as possible. Sledge looked up at the night sky and wondered if his family was looking at the same stars that he was. It was now 00:30 hours, and he knew at home his daughter and wife would be beginning their morning routine.

Off to the north he could see the occasional lights of civilian aircraft and wondered what and where the people on board were going. It was like being a bird with its wings clipped, thought Sledge. He was a flyer, and that was where he belonged. Forty thousand feet and shooting through the clouds like a dolphin playing in the waves. There he was a warrior, but not on the ground. Here, he was out of his element.

Unknown to Colonel Hammer at that moment was the

fact that thirty-five thousand feet above him, screaming towards the earth at one hundred and fifty six feet per second, eight individuals from his own country were on their way to take him back to the family that he was dreaming about.

17 ARRIVAL

The night above Korea was calm and clear, almost peaceful as Chris fell through twenty thousand feet. There was a slight breeze blowing towards the objective, which was a definite plus for the Nighthawks, but as with anything in life, there must be a balance, and with the blessing of a breeze came the curse of a clear sky and full moon. If the soldiers below had night vision goggles, which they probably did, thought Chris, the full moon and clear sky would make the team infinitely more visible. However, it also gave Chris and the other members of the Nighthawks the ability to make out more shapes and shadows from a higher altitude without wasting the batteries in their own night vision goggles while allowing them to see their target valley at a distance that would make their approach much more accurate.

Chris looked at his altimeter, and once again began his ritual of counting down the feet as he fell, saying a prayer that his chute would open correctly the first time. This time however, Chris tossed in another prayer, just in case someone was listening, that they would find Colonel Hammer right away and be able to get out undetected.

In the valley below, Captain Rhee looked out across the sleeping countryside, and hoped that Sgt. Kim's men were at least a little more vigilant than before. After this is all over, thought Rhee, you and I, Sgt. Kim, are going to have a little talk. Rhee picked up his radio. "Sgt. Kim, status, over." There was no response. Damn, what now? "Sgt. Kim, this is Captain Rhee, what is your status please." The radio was silent for a few seconds and then crackled to life.

"All secure. Nothing to report." Sgt. Kim responded.

Having radio trouble again Kim? Captain Rhee thought to himself as he answered. "Very well. I want you to check in with me every thirty minutes. Copy."

"Yes sir, every thirty minutes. Sgt. Kim out."

That should keep you awake.

Sgt. Kim put the radio back in its case and continued his search into the forest, constantly moving west to search for the pilot.

The Nighthawks pulled their chutes as the cue came over the radio from SSgt. Hecht, and again the world stopped. This time however, it was different. There was no joy of floating. No feeling of playfulness. No feeling of total freedom. Instead it was more like a feeling of being totally exposed. Nakedness. As if everyone below knew they were coming and were waiting for them. Chris wondered how much of it was in his imagination, and how much was instinct.

They had opened their chutes at a much lower altitude than over the Nevada desert and the ground came up to meet them faster. Chris reached around and unhooked his gear tether so that it would hit the ground before him, avoiding the possibility of being harmed by landing with an extra fifty pounds of equipment.

The night had been too quiet for Colonel Hammer, and the lack of any action combined with the lack of sleep, started to play tricks with his mind. To stay focused he had started staring at the stars through the branches of his burrow, wondering if his wife and daughter would see the same stars if they looked up at their own sky. He had actually found a constellation that he recognized in the northern part of the sky and as he tried to remember the name of it, a dark shadow, a cloud probably, for the briefest of moments seemed to take the constellation from the sky. Probably just the lack of sleep catching up to you old boy. He thought to himself as he again focused on the stars of the night sky and let sleep win for the first time in twenty-eight hours.

When all of the Nighthawks were on the ground and the parachutes and HALO gear had been concealed properly, the team huddled to get a quick head count.

"Welcome to Korea, boys." SSgt. Hecht declared as he approached the huddle, "Let's see how far we have to hike."

Chris pulled out the GPS receiver and plotted their exact location, give or take a few feet. They were exactly three-quarters of a mile north of the crash site, and had good cover on either side of the clearing

"We're about three-quarters of a mile north, Mike. If we move slowly we could be there in about an hour."

"All right, everybody give your gear one last check, we'll move out A.S.A.P." SSgt. Hecht unpacked the encrypted satellite uplink and made the call to "Grover" back at Home Base, to let Colonel Mulgrave know that the Muppets had landed safely and were proceeding to the objective in a few minutes. After receiving the all clear and being told that the extraction helicopters would be on station and standing by, Mike repacked the satellite dish and addressed the members of the team. "All right guys, let's do it. We'll travel in a two fire team element, strong side right, towards the clearing. Let's take it slow and careful. Have your mics set on voice activated, and make it as sensitive as possible--if anyone sees anything, I want everyone to hear about it. Okay, form up, let's go find us a pilot." Mike smiled and moved towards the point. The Nighthawks divided into a two fire team element, which was basically two separate teams consisting of four men each. Each member checked his microphone to make sure that it was set at its most sensitive setting, and did a quick radio check.

"Nighthawk Leader, Nighthawk Three, radio check."

"Nighthawk Three, Nighthawk Leader, five by five."

"Nighthawk Leader, Four, radio check."

"Four, Nighthawk Leader, five by five."

Each member followed in sequence until all had checked in, and then the two teams began their movement towards the original crash site of Colonel Hammer's F-22.

In Washington, General Mitchell was looking at the clock on his wall that had been set to North Korean time, thinking that the team should just about be there by now, as the Communications Sergeant knocked on the frame of his office door.

"General, Colonel Mulgrave just called, Rescue Team Alpha is on the ground and proceeding to the objective. They should be there within the hour."

"Thank you Sergeant, call and verify that the helicopters are on station. I don't want those boys in there waiting for a ride out."

"Yes sir." The Sergeant turned and went back to the communication center to complete the General's orders as General Mitchell called the President to update him on the progress of the operation.

The voice came through Chris's earpiece and made him jump slightly.

"Nighthawk Leader, Nighthawk Six, have movement eleven o'clock your position, looks like fifty meters. Copy?" The entire team froze and scanned the area with their night vision goggles.

SSgt. Hecht replied. "Copy that, have visual. Unless you guys want venison tonight, don't fire. Thanks Six." The deer came out from behind the bush and bolted across the clearing into the forest on the other side. The two fire teams remained still and listened for anything that the deer might have spooked in the way of North Koreans. The crickets and creatures of the forest resumed their orchestrations, but other than that and the beating hearts of the Nighthawks, the night was silent.

Sergeant Kim looked at his watch and rubbed his brow. It was now 01:00 hours and he had been conducting the unauthorized search for the past four hours without any luck. The men of his squad still didn't know that they were disobeying a direct order by conducting the search, and even believed that the order to leave the north part of the valley had come from the Captain himself. Sgt. Kim knew that there would be no way for Captain Rhee to find out, unless he for some odd reason sent a runner and even that would be unlikely. Kim had been more than vigilant in his thirty minute checks. No, the only way Rhee would find out, would be if I found the pilot, and then it wouldn't matter would it? Kim thought to himself as he looked up at the early morning sky.

There was a light breeze blowing and not a cloud in the sky as he peered up at the thousands of dots of light in the dark blue velvet. Are you looking at the same sky, American? Or are you in a hole hiding? Kim looked around at the shadows of the forest and listened to the crickets and other life, trying to find any sound that might be unnatural. There was none. Just the sound of a North Korean night. Damn! Where the hell are you?

The Nighthawks moved swiftly and silently through the forest, and Chris looked at his watch. They had only left the drop zone forty minutes ago, and at this rate would be at the crash site in another ten.

Chris whispered into his microphone. "Nighthawk Leader, Nighthawk Three. Possible wired area, maybe we should take it slow."

"Copy that Three, good point. Guys, let's keep that in the back of our minds. Play it safe. We're only ten out so start looking sharp. We can encounter any moment now." Mike took a deep breath as the image of hostile forces returning fire flashed through his mind. Maybe it would be like Chris had said. Get in get out, nobody the wiser. God I hope so...

"All Nighthawks, Nighthawk Leader, break into single fire teams. Let's start leapfrogging." Simultaneously, Mike gave the hand and arm signal for the order he was transmitting.

The Nighthawks split into their two separate units and started to leapfrog through the forest. One team going forward while the other team provided cover in case of contact. The movement was slower than if the team had proceeded in a line formation, but much more safe. Chris looked once again at his watch. 01:25 hours, right on schedule.

It might have been the lack of sleep, the tension of looking for something that couldn't be found, or just plain inexperience. But for whatever the reason Private Yim Yumin, just two months out of indoctrination training and on his first point assignment in a night forest, opened fire as the shadow crossed in front of his path. The report of the rifle shot echoed through the valley and at once three different teams and one pilot, in two different languages, were frantically trying to figure out what the hell had just happened.

"What the hell was that?" SSgt. Hecht asked as the entire team of Nighthawks froze.

"Nighthawk Leader, Nighthawk Three, Ak-47 fire. Sounds about three mikes to the west, copy?"

"Suggestions anyone?"

"Nighthawk Leader, Nighthawk Alpha, we don't know what that was about, I vote that we proceed to the original objective."

SSgt. Hecht now had one of the most delicate decisions of his career. If the Nighthawks proceeded to their original objective, and the shot was at Colonel Hammer, they would be going farther away from him when he needed them the most. If, on the other hand they stopped to investigate the shot and it had nothing to do with Colonel Hammer, the time wasted chasing wild sounds could be detrimental to the success of the mission. Mike looked up at the stars and searched for an answer.

"Proceed to the original destination, I repeat, proceed to the original destination copy."

Each of the Nighthawks radioed their acknowledgment and the team again started through the forest towards the site of Colonel Hammer's crash, each one hoping in their hearts that the shot they heard had nothing to do with their objective.

Captain Rhee looked in the direction of the shot. It was nowhere near the northern end of the valley where Sgt. Kim's men were, unless, thought Rhee, Sgt. Kim was not where he was supposed to be. Of course, Rhee shook his head, why doesn't that surprise me. Captain Rhee was almost screaming as he keyed the radio's microphone. "Sgt. Kim, what's your location, over."

"Northern end of the valley as instructed, sir."

Captain Rhee gritted his teeth and shook his head. You're mine Kim, you're mine.

"That's affirmative, I want you to send a two man team to recon the area that the shot came from, and report back to me at once, over."

The reply that came back was slightly terse and Captain Rhee smiled as he heard the stress in Sgt. Kim's voice.

"Yes sir, a two man team, copy that."

Captain Rhee turned to the soldier with him. "Leave two men with Stingers here in the southern end of the valley for the ambush and have everyone else come with me. Have them assemble here from their positions immediately."

The soldier saluted and ran off to give the message to the other members of the ambush team.

Rhee looked up at the stars in the night sky and swore at the incompetence that was still prevalent in some sections of his beloved country, and the inability of some to follow orders with discipline. There were still those who, instead of working hard and finding a satisfaction in that, wanted to live an "idle life", the Korean wish of good fortune. They had been the ones during the revolution that believed Communism would provide them with everything, that they would indeed attain the centuries old salutation of a life of leisure, with the state providing everything. It was a false hope and it had been some of the great leaders that had influenced Rhee as a child with their speeches of finding total satisfaction in hard work. That hard work was important for the survival of his country, and with the hard work came discipline and reward. No Kim, would never be like him, he would always be weak, and there was no place in his country for weak men, was there? No place at all, thought Rhee as a shooting star streaked across the night sky.

When all of the men, except those staying behind for the ambush, had assembled, Captain Rhee started working his way back up to the northern end of the valley. If Kim is there, fine. If not however, it will be the end of an already short career, thought Captain Rhee as the group moved through the forest, the same way they had entered.

Sgt. Kim looked at the dead deer in the middle of the trail and cursed. The combined bad luck of the deer startling the young soldier, and the worse luck of an inexperienced youth reacting hastily by firing his weapon, had brought all his thoughts of a promotion to a startling halt. He knew that Captain Rhee would be sending someone to the northern end of the valley to see if, indeed, Sgt. Kim and his men were where they said they were, and report back to him if not. And if Sgt. Kim and his men were not at the north end of the valley, any chance of a promotion would be gone.

Captain Rhee already suspected him for not calling in reinforcements and this added to that suspicion would be enough to ruin his already lackluster career. I have to get back to the north end of the valley, have to beat them back, and this time I have to make sure he believes the malfunctioning radio. Sgt. Kim looked at the rocks around his feet, and making sure that no one else saw him, turned off the radio and dropped it on one of them, shattering the top of the speaker. Kim picked up the radio and turned it on. It was still working, you just couldn't hear anything except static. Perfect. I'll tell Captain Rhee that we saw the American pilot moving through the woods and we had to give chase. We tried to contact him but our radio was broken. What else could I have done? Pleased with himself and his story, Sgt. Kim gave a slight smile and then called out to his men. "All right, everyone form up. We just got orders to get back to the northern end of the valley as soon as possible, and that's exactly what we're going to do." Sgt. Kim looked up at the night sky and wondered how much time he had.

The sleep that Colonel Hammer allowed to take over his body had immediately let his mind escape his current situation and allowed him to be in the arms of his wife and little girl once again. The dream took his mind back to a picnic the three of them had enjoyed in the park, on a bright spring day, when the shot shattered the current image in his mind and brought him back to reality with a cold sweat running down his forehead. He was still groggy from the sleep and had no idea if the shot he heard was meant for him or not. Sledge quickly scanned the surrounding area to see if any soldiers were in the immediate forest. The only sounds that Sledge could focus on was the sound of his own heart throbbing within his ears.

The Nighthawks moved quickly through the forest and came to a small clearing in the trees, about a quarter mile from the crash site, regrouping to go over their plan one more time. SSgt. Hecht took the radio out from his backpack and tried to contact Colonel Hammer. "Burner One Burner One, this is Nighthawk Leader, do you copy?" Silence.

"Burner One Burner One, this is Rescue Team Alpha, the Nighthawks, do you copy?" Again the air was filled with only the sounds of the forest.

"Okay guys, this is it. We go in. Team Two secures the perimeter and searches for the film from the gun camera. Team One finds Burner One and radios the Blackhawks for extraction. Any questions?" SSgt. Hecht looked at the other members of the Nighthawks as they gave one final check to their equipment, put on their night vision goggles and nodded their agreement. "All right, let's do it. Nighthawk Alpha you have Team Two, let's go."

The two teams again leap frogged towards the objective and came to the edge of the clearing, in view of the crash site. SSgt. Hecht took out the portable satellite dish and erected it inside a small bush at the edge of the clearing. Now the Nighthawks could communicate securely with Home Base by just changing the frequencies on their individual radios.

The two soldiers that had been stationed there by Captain

Rhee were pacing back and forth, again smoking cigarettes, trying to fight off the boredom. Little did they know that their prayers to end the boredom would be answered in just a few short moments.

SSgt. Hecht looked into the clearing and cursed.

"Nighthawk Six, Nighthawk Three, I have two at one o'clock. I need those two taken out with as little noise as possible."

"Copy that. Give us five minutes to get to an optimal position, then they're toast."

SSgt. Hecht looked at his watch. "Ten-four, five mikes, but that's all you get, any more time and those helicopter pilots are going to start getting nervous."

"No sweat Mike, I couldn't ask for a better sight picture than the cigs." Sgt. Ross said as he gave the thumbs up and he and the other sniper followed the tree line to get a closer view of the crash site. The other members of the Nighthawks crawled under the bushes and watched.

The two snipers also carried night vision, or Starlight scopes on their JARs, and as Chris looked through the scope at the soldier standing the farthest away from the crash site. He was struck by how the picture in his eye resembled a high tech video game. Except in his heart Chris knew that by squeezing the trigger of his rifle, he would not be ending the life of few pieces of electronic data, he would be ending the life of a man with a mother, father, and possibly a family of his own. He also knew that if given the opportunity, the soldier would do the exact same thing to him, and probably wouldn't have given it a second thought. "Nighthawk Six, Three. Do you have good target?"

"That's a roger Three. Positive target."

"Ten-four on my mark then. Three-Two-One." On one both snipers took a deep breath and held, as they slowly squeezed the trigger of their rifles, each seeing in the scope of their weapon their targets go limp and fall simultaneously.

Colonel Hammer was still scanning the area when his eyes were drawn to the red glow of the freshly lit cigarettes at the crash site. You rookies will never learn will you? Sledge thought as both soldiers paced back and forth. Never thinking about what you're doing.

Colonel Hammer watched as both soldiers cigarettes fell to the ground. Both soldiers falling like puppets whose strings had been cut.

Holy shit!!! What the fuck was that ?!! It was then that the thought first crossed Sledge's mind, Maybe it's the cavalry. Shit. Sledge grabbed the emergency radio from his vest and turned on the power. He was immediately rewarded with the sound of another American voice.

"Burner One, Burner One, this is Nighthawk Leader, do you copy?"

Sledge could hardly control his relief and desperately wanted to run into the clearing to find his would be rescuers. Go slow Sledge, go slow.

"Burner One, Burner One this is Nighthawk Leader, do you copy?"

Sledge took a deep breath and keyed the mike. "Nighthawk Leader, this is Burner One. I read you five by five, over."

"Ten-four Colonel, we're a rescue team and we've come to

take you home, copy? Prepare to authenticate. Do you still have your authentication sheet?"

Colonel Hammer frantically searched his flight suit. "Ten-four Nighthawk. Waiting for authentication."

"Copy that sir. I read you. Echo-Tango-Foxtrot-Alpha-Seven-One-Seven. I repeat, Echo-Tango-Foxtrot-Alpha-Seven-One-Seven, do you copy?"

Sledge watched as the sequence he was hearing matched the sequence on his card. and tears started to well in his eyes. "Copy that, I have a good authentication and I read you Sierra Six. Welcome to North Korea."

"Thank you sir. We are a quarter mile out from the crash site, what is your location?"

"I'm in the tree line just east of the crash, copy?"

"Copy that sir. Do you require medical attention?"

"That's affirmative, I think I busted up my ankle pretty bad. I can still move, but it's slow."

"Ten-four on that sir. We'll be approaching from the north. A team should reach you in about five minutes, copy?"

"Ten-four, five minutes from the north."

"Ten-four, see you in a bit."

As Sledge put the radio down, the emotions of the last two days finally hit him. He wasn't going to die in this god forsaken country, without ever seeing his little girl again. He was going to see her in the next day or two. And as the thought of seeing his little princess again flooded his mind, Colonel Hammer, husband and father, put his face in his hands and cried.

SSgt. Hecht turned the radio frequency to contact Home Base and keyed the mike. "Grover, this is Muppet Leader, we have contact, I repeat we have contact. Need helicopter evac at crash site coordinates. Copy?"

Colonel Mulgrave jumped up from the desk so hard he almost caught his knee on the edge of the table. Hot damn, they got him! "Copy that Muppet Leader. Need evac at crash site. Blackhawks are on station fifteen minutes out. Copy?"

"Copy that, fifteen mikes."

"Any resistance Muppet Leader?"

"Two soldiers at crash site. Sniper practice, copy?"

"Copy two at crash site, no trouble. Let's hope it stays that way. Over."

"That's a big ten-four sir. Muppet Leader out." Mike switched the frequency back to Colonel Hammer frequency and clipped the radio to his load bearing vest. Mike took off his night vision goggles and looked up at the stars above. Yes, let's hope it stays that way.

The two teams separated as Team Two went to secure the perimeter of the crash site, and Team One proceeded to find Colonel Hammer.

Captain Rhee's men reached the edge of the clearing just as Team Two of the Nighthawks had finished a sweep of the area.

Nighthawk Six was the first of the team to see the North Koreans as they approached from the south. "Nighthawk Alpha, Nighthawk Six, movement at one o'clock, two hundred meters, copy."

"Copy that Nighthawk Six. Team Two do not engage, I repeat if at all possible, do not engage. Let's see where they go. Nighthawk Leader, this is Alpha, we have inbound hostiles copy? We're going to try not to engage, I repeat, trying not to engage."

Mike Hecht's heart skipped a beat. "Copy that, Alpha. Be

advised that evac is inbound, fifteen minutes out, if they're still in the area when the choppers arrive it's going to be like world war three getting out of here. Team One standing by."

"That's a big ten-four Mike." SSgt. Miller adjusted his night vision goggles to get a better view of the North Koreans as they approached the crash site.

Captain Rhee looked at the crash site and wondered, Where the hell are the soldiers? Damn Sgt. Kim's men, they probably went off on their own too. Rhee keyed the mike on his radio. "Crash site, this is Captain Rhee, what's your status over?" There was no response.

"Crash site, this is Captain Rhee, acknowledge please." Again, nothing.

Captain Rhee turned to Corporal Koh. "Go to the Crash site and find those two soldiers, when you find out their whereabouts, call me on their radio." The soldier saluted and ran off towards the crash site.

"Nighthawk Six, Nighthawk Alpha. Lone target approaching crash site. I need him taken out, copy? He can't get to the crash site."

"I can't get a good picture, copy?"

"Well get one fast, or we're toast."

"Ten-four" Nighthawk Six took off his night vision goggles and raised his weapon with the starlight scope to his eye. The North Korean was moving erratically and not providing him with a clear shot. Missing would be worse than not firing at all. Fuckin' A' stay still, thought Nighthawk Six as he tried to get a good target.

The soldier arrived at the crash site and saw what was left of his two comrades. The head of each body had been nearly separated by the force of the high powered sniper rifles. Both now lay in a pool of dark colored mud. He couldn't believe what he was seeing as he brought his whistle up to his lips and blew. It would be the last sound that he would ever make.

Sgt. Hinkle saw him raise his hand with the whistle and pulled the trigger, good target or not. The bullet found its target on the right side of the head just above the ear and dropped the soldier to the earth, like the wind blowing a leaf. The shot however, was not in time, and the sound of the whistle screamed through the night air.

The sound of the whistle reached Captain Rhee's ears within seconds and all that he had feared had come true. Somehow the Americans had gotten in. Damn. "Everybody take cover." Captain Rhee peered out into the darkness tried to see if he could see any of the intruders of his homeland. "Give me a set of night vision goggles ASAP."

"We only have two pair sir, and the batteries are dead."

"What about replacement batteries?" Rhee asked, the anger starting to show in his voice.

"We don't have any sir."

Captain Rhee shook his head in disbelief. Damn incompetence. Without the night vision goggles it would be nearly impossible to see the Americans, who more than likely did have night vision goggles, and they definitely had extra batteries.

"All right, use a flare. At least we will be able to see them for a moment."

The soldier pulled a slap flare out of his pack and went to the edge of the clearing, where he proceeded to fire it into the night sky. The illumination was the equivalent of two-hundred and fifty thousand candles and lit the clearing in an eerie bright white light.

Fortunately Team Two of the Nighthawks had seen the soldier step into the clearing to fire the slap flare and were able to find cover from the searching eyes of the North Koreans before the flare fired.

Damn. Captain Rhee swore to himself. He had given away his position to the Americans with nothing in return. That will be my first and only tactical mistake. How could I have been so impatient? Rhee picked up the radio and called Sgt. Kim. "Sgt. Kim, this is Captain Rhee, come in, over." Again for the third time tonight there was no response and the anger inside Rhee's mind exploded into pure rage. "Sgt. Kim this is Captain Rhee, if you don't answer your radio I will personally come up there, hold the tribunal, and kill you myself, now where are you!" Again there was no reply, just static. Damn you Kim.

"All right listen up. It looks like we won't be getting any help from Sgt. Kim, so it appears that we alone are going to engage the Americans until reinforcements arrive. They must not be allowed to escape with the downed pilot. They got in here, but they still have to get out, and that means that they still need helicopters. We can take care of those when they arrive, we still have a few stingers left, but first we need to stop the Americans from succeeding in this clear act of war. They have sent an invasion force into our homeland, and we are going to stop them. Stay in the trees and engage from a safe distance. Take out as many as you can with sniper fire. Dismissed." The North Koreans moved slowly, cautiously down the tree line to the site of the crashed American plane.

Colonel Hammer looked through the darkened trees to try and see any of the team that was here to rescue him, and could see nothing. No movement, no sounds, nothing that he hadn't already seen for the past hours. As he peered out into the clearing a hand touched him on his shoulder, sending a shock down his spine.

Sgt. Ross looked at the most happy face that he had ever seen in his entire life. "Colonel Hammer, Sgt. Ross of the Nighthawks. Can I take a quick look at your ankle sir?"

"Damn, you guys are good. I didn't even see you."

"That's what they pay us for. Now how about letting me look at that ankle?"

"Huh? What? Oh. It will be fine, don't worry about it, just get me the hell out of here."

"As soon as we can Colonel, just sit tight, the choppers are on their way now." Chris keyed the mike on his radio. "Nighthawk Leader, Nighthawk Three, I have the package and the area's secure, copy?"

"Ten-Four Nighthawk Three, we're coming in. Tell the Colonel that his taxi is ten minutes out, copy?"

"Copy that. I think he heard. Over."

The rest of Team One now entered the little clearing that Sgt. Ross and Colonel Hammer were occupying

Chris looked at his friend across the clearing, "See Mike, get in, get the Colonel, and then get out. They don't even know that we're here."

Mike's face looked grim. "They know we're here they just can't find us."

Sgt. Kim, with his men, entered the north end of the clearing expecting to see the Captain sitting there waiting for him. Instead there was just the sound of the Korean night and the stars above. Well, that's a good sign, maybe it'll be all right after all. I can just sit here in the clearing and claim that the radio had been broken all along. He again set his team up in their original ambush positions and sat back to wait.

SSgt. Miller watched as the North Koreans edged their way closer and closer to his position. Damn this isn't pretty. Miller thought as he keyed the button at his side and whispered into the mike. "Nighthawk Leader, Nighthawk Alpha. We have inbound hostiles. They're heading straight for us Mike. They don't know our position yet, but they will once they step on us. You might have to move Team One into a position to flank them if things get ugly. Copy?"

"Copy that Nighthawk Alpha. We'll move up towards the north and cut across them from above." SSgt. Hecht turned to Colonel Hammer. "Do you think that you can stand to be on you own for a little while if we have to dance?"

Colonel Hammer smiled, "I've done okay so far."

"Copy that." SSgt. Hecht spoke into his mic. "Nighthawk Team One, form up and move to the north, we're going to flank the North Koreans just in case something happens with Team Two. Give them some cover. Move out."

Nighthawk Team One, once again left Colonel Hammer alone and isolated in a foreign land, and moved to a position north of Nighthawk Team Two.

Captain Rhee evaluated his situation as his team moved closer to the crash site. Without Sgt. Kim and the others he only had six men, and most of them were, in his opinion, poorly trained. They still had a few Stinger missiles and if they could get close enough, when the chopper came in for the pilot, they could use them to take out the chopper and the rescue team at the same time. It wouldn't be the same as a live pilot, but it would still give his government a big edge at the summit. Especially if the United States wanted to keep an embarrassing defeat quiet. The only problem was how close they could get without being spotted.

Nighthawk Team Two had formed a line perpendicular to the approaching North Koreans, and watched as the team progressed closer to their position. If that's not the worst luck. Why couldn't you have chosen another path? SSgt. Miller thought to himself as he brought his sights on one of the soldiers, just in case. Move away. Please move away.

Miller again whispered into the microphone of his radio. "Nighthawk Leader, Nighthawk Alpha, how far out are those choppers, over?"

"Nighthawk Alpha, stand by." Mike switched frequencies on his radio and called Home Base. "Grover, Grover, this is Muppet Leader. Over."

"Go ahead Muppet Leader, this is Grover."

"Roger. What's the ETA of inbound, over?"

"Stand by."

The silence over the radio was the worse sound that Mike could imagine as he waited for the answer and watched the Korean team move closer to Team Two.

"Muppet Leader, this is Grover. Inbound is five mikes out copy?"

"Ten-four Grover. Advise inbound that it could be a possible hot LZ copy? We have a possible hot LZ. Unfriendlies are getting close. Over."

"Ten-four Muppet Leader, will advise inbound, possible hot LZ." Colonel Mulgrave looked at the clock on the wall and bit his lower lip. "Good luck Muppet Leader, Grover out."

Mike again switched frequencies and called Team Two's leader. "Nighthawk Alpha, Nighthawk Leader, chopper is five out copy?"

"Copy that. Be advised Mike, it looks like they're carrying stingers, I repeat, they have Stingers, Copy?"

Fuck! what the hell else could go wrong, Mike thought as he looked at Chris and patted his stomach. "Copy that, Stinger missiles sighted. Looks like were going to have to take them out before the choppers get in here. Let's do it hard and fast, over. Nighthawk Six give me a report. What kind of targets do you have?"

"Nighthawk Leader, Nighthawk Six, I have one positive, one possible copy?"

"Copy that Six, tango. Let me call Home to let 'em know." Once again SSgt. Hecht switched frequencies to call Home Base. "Grover this is Muppet Leader, we're going to have to go hot, copy? We have to go hot. Hostiles have Stinger missiles and are moving towards the LZ."

Colonel Mulgrave traded looks with the two pilots that were in the communication center with him. Their eyes said the same thing. If the choppers landed they would be sitting ducks for Stingers, and all of this would be wasted lives. Colonel Mulgrave pushed the transmit button. "Copy that Muppet Leader, have visual on Stingers, going hot. You have my authorization to proceed. Copy?"

"Copy that Grover, talk to you in a bit."

"Ten-four Muppet Leader, Grover out."

Mike turned the frequency back to its original setting. "Nighthawk Alpha, Nighthawk Leader, we have authorization from Grover. Let's do it."

"Copy that Nighthawk Leader. Team Two prepare to engage on my command. Get a good site picture guys, I want this over before the choppers get in here. Nighthawk Leader, what is your position?"

"Nighthawk Alpha, Nighthawk Leader, we are in position to flank, copy? We are ninety degrees north of your location."

"Copy that, we'll shift fire on your command. Team Two, fire at will."

The Korean team was only twenty-five feet from the unseen Americans as the quiet night erupted with the sound of gunfire and three of Captain Rhee's men were hit immediately. For a split second Captain Rhee was frozen like a deer in a pair of headlights, the muzzle flashes from the American guns appearing right in front of him. When his mind again started working, he realized that three of his men had been killed immediately, the other three men had taken cover behind trees at the edge of the forest and were returning fire.

If there was a positive side to what had just happened was that now they could know how many Americans there were and where they were located. Captain Rhee dove behind a tree and counted the flashes from the intruder's weapons. Four Americans. Probably Marine Force Recon. As the rest of his men engaged the Americans, Rhee again called headquarters for reinforcements and was told that they were twenty minutes out, to sit tight and return fire for as long as possible. *If they had only listened to me sooner. I told them that there would be a rescue. They never understand.*

Captain Rhee looked out at the battle now taking place and tried to develop a strategy. At the moment his men were holding their own, which was pleasing to Rhee, since they were just a basic infantry unit facing the highly trained American Special Forces. The battle was basically a stand-off between the two forces, Captain Rhee's men dug in behind the trees in the forest and the Americans at the edge of the clearing still protected by the trees. Rhee knew that at this rate they would soon be out of ammunition before the reinforcements arrived, and then it wouldn't much matter how late they were. *If only I could make contact with Sgt.*

Kim, his team could flank the Americans within minutes. In a futile gesture, Captain Rhee again tried to reach Sgt. Kim on the radio.

The sound of gunfire spread across the valley in waves of echoes that reached Sgt. Kim's men with a start. Kim immediately knew that the sound was a mixture of AK-47 fire, and another type of weapon that more than likely belonged to an American rescue team. From the sounds of the exchange things were getting pretty hot down in the south, and Sgt. Kim for a brief second debated sending his team to help. Could still say that the radio was broken. But what about the gunfire? Would have to say I heard it, no, you have to go Kim, it's the honorable thing to do. Kim looked across the Korean night to the sounds of gunfire echoing through the valley, and decided to do not what his heart told him, which was to run, but to do what he would be less accountable for, and proceeded with his men toward the sounds of war.

The static that proceeded the radio message broke SSgt. Hecht's concentration on the task at hand. "Nighthawk Leader, Nighthawk Leader, this is Phoenix One and Two, one minute out of your location. I copy we have a hot LZ."

"Phoenix One that's a roger. Be advised they have active Stinger missiles, suggest you stay clear until we clean this up copy."

"Copy that Nighthawk Leader, we'll station one mile out, contact when ready, over."

"Ten-four Phoenix One. Nighthawk Alpha, Nighthawk

Leader did you copy that transmission? We need to get this over with. Copy?"

"That's affirmative. Listen Mike we're at a stand off here, but I don't think that they know of your existence, why don't we wake them up a little."

"Ten-four. We'll start from our position, shift your fire twenty degrees. Copy?"

"Copy. Twenty degrees."

"Team One this is it. Let's get those choppers in here. Chris what have you got?"

Chris looked through his starlight scope and was surprised at the good fortune of what he saw. "Nighthawk Leader, I have a positive target behind a tree, copy?"

"Ten-four Chris, go ahead and take him out. Team One when the his target is down move in. Team Two, on my command cease fire copy?"

"Nighthawk Alpha copy."

"Six copy."

"Seven copy"

"Eight copy."

Chris looked through the scope and again took a deep breath to ease his breathing, held it, and slowly squeezed the trigger of his weapon.

"Team Two cease fire! I repeat cease fire! Team One move."

Nighthawk Team One jumped up from their positions in the grass and ran towards the tree line opening fire as they went.

Captain Rhee was standing behind a tree trying to get a better look at the fire patterns, and possibly get a better fix on the aggressors' location, when the bullet screamed through the night air and entered his body in a burning white hot flash that ruptured his spinal cord and shattered his vertebrae. The impact of the shot knocked Captain Rhee on his side, looking towards the clearing, where he could see a second team of Americans approaching. Fool! How could I have overlooked the possibility of a second team.

Captain Rhee couldn't feel the pain in his legs and assumed that his legs were useless. He could see the approaching American and tried to reach for his weapon, but then found that his arms were useless as well. He was paralyzed. Fuck! Well, if you can't fight, at least you can stay alive. Rhee watched the American enter his field of vision and closed his eyes.

Sgt. Hoffman looked at the dead Korean soldiers and made a quick count. "Nighthawk Leader, I got six DOA copy? Six Dead."

"Copy that Four. Phoenix One, Nighthawk Leader area secure, copy? Area secure."

"Copy that Nighthawk leader. We're one mike out and will be there ASAP."

"Ten-four Phoenix One. Nighthawk Five, get Colonel Hammer. We're outa here."

The two UH-60 Blackhawk helicopters flew just above the tree tops as they crossed the North Korean countryside. For this mission each of the choppers carried a complement of three crew members from the 301st Special Operations

Squadron, a pilot, copilot, and a gunner manning a machine gun in the rear. The gunner scanned the mountainous area with night vision goggles for any sign of movement. The thought of Stinger missiles made the crew's blood run cold in their veins.

The Stinger was designed by the Americans as a portable anti-aircraft missile for use against Soviet jets, and played a big role in the security of South Korea, but against a slow moving helicopter there would be no contest. As with everything there was a certain amount of corruption in the South and a few of the missiles easily made their way into North Korean hands, where they were copied and developed for their own use. Although not as well made as the American version, it was enough to accomplish what it was designed for.

The UH-60 Blackhawk was a marvel of design. Bigger than the workhorse of the American military, the Bell UH-1 Huey, it held eleven troops instead of the Huey's four. If you took out the gunners on both aircraft, the Blackhawk would seat fifteen to the Huey's eight. Its top speed was two hundred and eighteen miles per hour, with a maximum range of two hundred and eighty-six miles and a endurance of two hours and forty-two minutes, which could be stretched in an emergency.

The Blackhawks skimmed over the mountain top and entered the valley which held the Nighthawks and the pilot that had been shot down the night before.

As Sgt. Kim and his men moved farther south down into

the valley, they could here the American helicopters in the distance and began running towards the crash site; desperately trying to get to the clearing before it would be too late to even fire a shot. Sgt. Kim knew that they still had a Stinger missile and if they could get in close enough they could take out the choppers on the ground and still be heroes. The lack of gunfire and the sounds of the choppers, told Sgt. Kim all he needed to know about the fate of Captain Rhee and his team. A smile came across Kim's face as a striking thought came to his mind. Well, it looks like you're in charge again. Still a chance to earn a promotion.

Captain Rhee watched helplessly as the two American helicopters landed in the clearing near the crash site, their rotors blowing dust and dirt into his face. It was a cruel form of torture to watch and not be able to do anything as the Americans boarded the two choppers with the downed American pilot. Captain Rhee cursed the actions that had brought him to this point.

Mike Hecht watched as the two choppers landed in the meadow. "Nighthawk Alpha, Nighthawk Leader, take Colonel Hammer with you on Phoenix One, Team One will egress on Phoenix Two copy?"

"That's a B-I-G ten-four Nighthawk Leader, elbows and asses to the choppers and a short ride home."

Team Two, helped Colonel Hammer into the Blackhawk, as Team One moved across the clearing to board Phoenix Two and prepared to take off.

As Phoenix Two started to lift off, Chris noticed a second

team of North Korean soldiers running into the clearing and pause to take aim with a Stinger missile. Chris jumped out of the helicopter, dived to the ground, and automatically fired two shots at the incoming threat.

Captain Rhee noticed the commotion and strained his eyes to see what was taking place. He could just barely make out Sgt. Kim and his men coming into the clearing. Sgt. Kim was in the lead with a Stinger missile. Sgt. Kim dropped to one knee and started to arm the missile to take out the chopper that was climbing into the night sky. As he pulled the safety pin on the unit, Captain Rhee watched as the American's bullet struck Sgt. Kim right between the eyes.

The other soldiers were firing blindly into the night sky with their automatic weapons, not even noticing in the confusion, the other chopper on the ground, whose gunner was just about to open fire and end the threat. It was over within seconds as the Blackhawk's gunner opened fire with his fifty caliber machine gun, literally cutting the North Korean soldiers in half.

"Nighthawk Three, Nighthawk Leader, Phoenix One is holding for you, disengage, copy? Disengage."

"Copy that Nighthawk Leader, catching a ride with Phoenix One." Chris got up and jumped into the back of the chopper as the pilot applied full power and climbed into the night sky. Both choppers cleared the Mountain and dropped to the top of the trees to sneak their way back out of the county.

The pilot of Phoenix One pressed the mike button on his flight stick. "Gentleman, this is your captain speaking, the stewardesses have turned off the no smoking sign and will be handing out refreshments in the aft compartments, you may now feel free to move about the compartment. Thank you for flying Phoenix airlines."

There were smiles and high five's as the Nighthawks flew above the tree tops on the way out of harm's way. Chris keyed the mike on his radio. "See that Mike, get in, get out, no problem."

"Copy that Chris, I guess the stomach can't always be right. By the way, nice shot back there. I think I owe you a beer for taking out that Stinger."

"Copy that."

Although he couldn't see his friend in the night sky, in his mind he could see Chris's smile. "Ten-four. Nighthawk Leader out."

SSgt. Hecht switched frequencies for one last time and called Home Base. "Grover this is Muppet Leader, do you copy?"

"Nice to hear your voice Muppet Leader. Status?"

"We have the package, and are on our way out, copy?"

Colonel Mulgrave smiled. "Copy that. Congratulations Mike. Give my best to the team. Over." Colonel Mulgrave sat down at his desk and lit his ceremonial cigar.

"Copy that, Muppet Leader out." Mike turned off the radio and stared out the window at the dark trees passing below.

Unknown to both teams, one of the bullets fired at random by the North Korean soldiers had found a home, barely grazing the tail rotor of Phoenix Two. Not enough to make any visible damage, just enough to start a hairline fracture on blade two of the stabilizer rotor system.

18 FRACTURES

The pressures caused by flying at full throttle in the hard air of low altitude caused the fracture to grow at an ever quickening pace. In the cockpit of Phoenix Two, the pilot started to feel a slight shudder in the flight control system. "Phoenix One this is Phoenix Two, be advised, I'm experiencing some slight buffeting in the joystick. I might have taken some damage back there in the valley, copy?"

"Copy that Phoenix Two. We're five minutes out from friendly territory, do you think it's a problem?"

"Phoenix One, I have no warning lights at this time, it's probably just damage to the frame. I'll keep you advised, Two out." The pilot took a look back at his passengers and had noticed that, having spent all of their adrenaline, the three of them had already fallen asleep. As he turned his attention back towards the front of the chopper, he pressed the intercom button on his stick to talk to the copilot. "I hope if I ever go down, these guys are still around to get me out."

The copilot nodded his head in agreement. "You and me both, buddy, you and me both."

"Phoenix Two, Phoenix One, turn to a heading of One-Four-Five, coming up on final waypoint. How's the shimmy? Over."

"Phoenix One, Phoenix Two, that's a roger, One-Four-Five. Shimmy's still there seems to be getting a little stronger, but it might just be the crosswinds."

"Ten-four Phoenix Two, be advised, only three minutes out."

Sgt. Ross looked out the window at the trees flying by below, and saw the black shadow that was the other Blackhawk flying slightly behind and to the left. He wondered what was happening inside the other chopper. If the rest of his team was doing the same thing that the team on Phoenix One was doing, sleeping. It had started with Colonel Hammer, who, finally out of danger, in the company of his own countrymen, had closed his eyes almost immediately. The rest of the team had followed suit as the adrenaline from the mission had started to wear off, and the fatigue from the stress took over. The only reason that Chris wasn't sleeping was his love of flight and everything that went with it. Occasionally, on the 737 flights up to Groom lake, he would sleep, but that was only because it was so often that it had become routine. But now, flying just above the tree tops at two hundred miles per hour, he couldn't turn his attention from the outside stimulus.

"Phoenix Two, Phoenix One, be advised we're coming up on the DMZ be alert for some action, copy?"

"Copy that Phoenix One, have visual on DMZ."

Chris had switched his radio frequency so that he could listen to the pilots, and looked forward to seeing the DMZ. Ahead was a winding strip of barren dirt, cut out of the forest on either side and framed by a chain-link fence with lights on both sides. Barbed wire was strewn in the center and it reminded Chris slightly of the pictures he had seen on the areas just outside the wall in Germany. Except this wasn't in Germany and the people on both sides didn't have a wall to block the other's view. Just the fence and on the other side, soldiers. Soldiers warning you not to enter their little piece of earth.

The Blackhawks screamed above the DMZ at fifty feet and Chris watched as the barren earth passed beneath his chopper.

"Phoenix Two, Phoenix One, climbing to altitude, copy?"

"That's a roger, climbing to friendly skies."

As the pilot of Phoenix Two adjusted the cyclic and throttle to take them to the higher altitude the warning light on the control panel came on and the urgent beeping of the audio alarm filled the cabin.

"Phoenix One, Phoenix Two, be advised, I have a tail rotor warning light and the buffeting just got noticeably worse. I'm gonna have to set her down. Copy? I'm putting her down."

"Copy that Phoenix Two. There's a clearing slightly east of our position. Go ahead and put her down, we'll land and pick you up if necessary. Over."

"That's a roger Phoenix One, setting down in that clearing."

The pilot reached down to adjust the throttle. Unfortunately, it was the exact moment that the fracture in tail rotor blade number two decided to become a crack. The stress caused by the imbalance of the rotor blades caused the rest of the blade to disintegrate almost immediately. The tail rotor broke apart, and without any stabilizing system the torque of the main rotor blades caused the Blackhawk to spin violently out of control, tumbling like a rock into the earth below. Although he tried there was absolutely nothing that the pilot of Phoenix Two could do.

Chris watched in horror as the helicopter with the rest of his team and his best friend exploded in a bellowing fire ball on the ground below.

The explosion and confusion in the cockpit of Phoenix One, awoke the rest of the Nighthawks and Colonel Hammer. All looked out aghast at the burning wreckage below as Phoenix One circled the impact site.

SSgt. Miller picked up the radio and placed an urgent call to Home Base. "Grover, Grover, this is Muppet Alpha, over."

Colonel Mulgrave and the two pilots in the communication center traded questioning looks at the tension in the unexpected voice of Muppet Alpha, second in command.

"Go ahead Muppet Alpha, what's the trouble?"

"Be advised Phoenix Two just went down in South Korean territory. I repeat. Phoenix Two just went in. We are now circling and are preparing to land."

The three faces in the control center went white. It had gone so well, almost perfect. The team had even handled a tricky situation with the North Koreans and came out smelling like a rose. So close to total success, thought Colonel Mulgrave as he reached down to the table and crushed out his cigar.

"Copy Muppet Alpha, Team One's chopper went down in friendly territory, no survivors, seven dead."

"Negative Grover, Nighthawk Three had to do some emergency work and missed his flight, he's on board with us, copy? Only six possible dead."

"Ten-Four, Keep this channel open, Copy?"

"Copy Grover."

Phoenix One landed as close to the impact site as possible and the Nighthawks were out the door with fire extinguishers before it had even settled.

The twisted wreckage of Phoenix Two was in a relatively compact circle and the Nighthawks had the fire extinguished within a few minutes. The scene was unbearable as Chris walked around the wreckage looking at the six twisted bodies. All were dead, dying on impact and Chris hoped that they had all been asleep like the team in his chopper, so that they wouldn't have been aware of what was happening.

"Muppet Alpha, this is Grover, Over."

"Go ahead Grover."

"Muppet Alpha there has been a rescue chopper sent out from Kunsan to recover the bodies, they should be there in five minutes. You and the rest of the Nighthawks are to recover anything that would tie those men to the team and exit the area. I repeat, you are not to make contact with the rescue chopper, we already have Phoenix Two covered. Copy?"

"Grover, this is Muppet Alpha, could you repeat last. You want us to leave them here?"

"That's affirmative Muppet Alpha, you are not to be in the area when the other chopper gets there, and you are to make sure nothing is left to connect Phoenix Two to the Nighthawks. Copy?"

"Copy that Grover, Nighthawks out."

SSgt. Miller shook his head in disbelief. "All right guys you heard it. Let's sanitize the area and get out of here."

Chris looked at the body of the person who was the best friend he had in his entire life and tried not to let the tears come as he took off the necklace that he knew would be there. The Nighthawks were supposed to leave all personal effects on the Gulfstream before the jump, but Chris knew that Mike would be wearing the gold cross and chain with his wedding ring attached. Sarah had given him the cross when they were dating and Mike always said that he wanted to carry a piece of Sarah with him for good luck. Chris put the necklace in his pocket. Damn it Mike... Go in peace my friend... Chris got up and joined the rest of the Nighthawks as they made sure that there were no clues to be left behind, and again boarded the Blackhawk and headed for safety. Chris watched out the window as the pilot applied full throttle and Phoenix One lifted off of the South Korean soil and flew off into the night sky.

As they gained altitude, Chris could see the wreckage become smaller and smaller until it was just a dot in his memory. The only sound on the rest of the flight was the sound of Muppet Alpha telling Grover that the mission was accomplished and the sound of the main rotors cutting through the wind as Phoenix One headed towards their destination of Kunsan AFB to return at least one man to his family.

Colonel Mulgrave picked up the secure phone in his office and contacted the control center at the Pentagon. He looked up at the clock on the wall, it was 16:00 hours in Washington, still enough time to reach General Mitchell before the end of the day, and through him, personally brief the President before he left for the North Korean Summit.

The call was routed directly to General Mitchell's office and the red phone on the corner of his desk started ringing. General Mitchell answered it on the first ring. "This is General Mitchell."

"General it's Colonel Mulgrave, I have some bad news."

General Mitchell's rubbed his face with his hand. "What happened Paul?"

"Colonel Hammer is fine, he's out and already on his way to Kunsan. Phoenix Two went down sir. All on board were killed, we lost six men, three from the 301st SOG, and three of the Nighthawks."

"Where did Phoenix Two go down?" General Mitchell asked as he rubbed his temples.

"South Korea. It appears that they received some damage to the tail rotor during the extraction, and it gave way as soon as they tried to go to altitude over South Korea."

"Well, you have my condolences Paul, I'm sure the team is feeling the loss. I'll brief the President. Anything else?"

"No sir, we covered the crash of Phoenix Two with the story that they were testing advanced avionics and that the Nighthawks were civilians. Kunsan will be sending their bodies to Nellis right away, and the two pilots and gunner will be sent back to Kadena in Japan to join their unit."

"Good work Russ. I'll put in a word for you for the quick thinking."

"General, I'd prefer that you put in a word for the guys who lost their lives, they're the ones who did the work."

"I'll see what I can do Paul. Give my regards to the rest of the team."

"Will do General."

General Mitchell heard the click on the other end of the line and hung up the phone on his desk. He looked out his window again at the green hills of Arlington and winced at the thought of more stones added to that monument of great patriots. Was he worth it, or was he worth it because of their friendship? In his heart he knew the answer. Yes, they were friends but that wasn't the reason. Colonel Donald Hammer was an American risking his life behind enemy lines, to bring information that would give his country the truth it needed to expose, and that American couldn't be found and tortured and paraded in front of the press like some kind of wild animal, having his life eventually ended in an execution. Not to mention the political ramifications, important to the President, but less so to the General. No, with the General it was more a matter of honor, of doing what was right. It was the same thing that the men who had died believed in. It was the reason they were there in the first place because they thought it was right. Somehow that thought consoled him as he picked up the phone and called for his driver to meet him out front as soon as possible.

The President was in the Oval Office taking care of some last minute business before he left for the Korean Summit, when his secretary buzzed him on the intercom. "Sir, General Mitchell requests to see you immediately, shall I send him in?"

"Yes Mary, send him in."

General Mitchell entered the Oval Office and came in front of the President's oak desk.

"I hope you have good news for me Paul. I'm just about

to leave for the summit, anything I should know about?"

General Mitchell opened the folder and began his briefing. "At 14:00 hours local time today Rescue Team Alpha secretly entered North Korea, and after engaging North Korean forces, extracted Colonel Hammer. There are eight confirmed North Korean casualties. Phoenix One and Two, the two Blackhawk helicopters, egressed the area under small arms fire, and Phoenix Two received damage, unknown at the time, to its tail rotor. While progressing to altitude over the DMZ, the tail rotor on Phoenix Two shattered, rendering the chopper uncontrollable. Phoenix Two then crashed on South Korean soil, resulting in the death of all six on board. Three Nighthawks, two pilots and the gunner from the 301st.

A rescue unit from Kunsan was dispatched to the area and a cover story was issued that the Blackhawk was engaged in classified avionics testing at the time of the crash and that everyone other than the pilot, copilot, and gunner were civilian. The bodies are currently being flown to Nellis for burial. Colonel Hammer is in good condition at Kunsan hospital. Unfortunately the gun film was destroyed, so the NSA has recalibrated one of their satellites and should have pictures of the Nuclear Weapons Center transmitted to Air Force One while you're in flight."

President McKallister let out a long deep sigh. "Is there anything that I can do for the families of the six men who lost their lives?"

"Well sir, you could authorize me to award them the Meritorious Service Medal, however, all the awards and documents would be classified. The only people who would know that they received them would be people briefed on the mission."

The President turned toward the Rose Garden. "So, in other words, anything I do wouldn't matter, it would just ease my conscience."

General Mitchell could feel the remorse in the President's voice. It was strange how a man could make life and death decisions all day and yet still be effected by the outcome of those decisions. "Well sir, it would mean something to the team to know that their members aren't forgotten."

"Very well, award them the Meritorious Service Medal, and give my regards to the rest of the team. I want you to be at the funeral, make it part of a morale tour or something, but I want the team to know of our support. If that's all General, I have a summit to get to."

"Yes sir, I'll catch a flight tomorrow."

"Good. And Paul, if you need my help on anything with this just call, you know where I'll be. I'm sure I'll hear about our little escapade from the North Korean delegation at the summit." The President smiled. "Of course I'll deny everything."

19 REUNIONS

After a quick examination at Kunsan AFB, Colonel Hammer had been allowed to catch the first medical evac plane back to the States. Now, after the long flight he found himself in the more familiar surroundings of the Nellis AFB hospital. The Nighthawks, he knew, had already returned to Area 51, without much fanfare or recognition and Colonel Hammer promised himself that when he returned to the base just north in the desert, he would find the secret team and give his personal thanks. He wanted to make sure that they knew that someone appreciated the job they did, someone appreciated it very much.

The sun was shining through the window and Sledge wondered if he had bumped into any of them during his day to day activities at the base. Probably, thought Sledge. As the thought crossed Sledge's mind the door to his room opened and the little princess that had kept Sledge going through all the rough times, ran across the room and jumped on the bed, oblivious to the cast on his ankle. "Daddy, Daddy you're back, you're back! Can we go see a movie and get ice cream?"

It was going to be tough for his wife to learn that she wasn't any longer the most important woman in his life, but as he caught her look he realized that she already knew.

"Of course we can pumpkin. Just wait until I'm out of here and I'll race you to the bottom of a banana split."

Marie Hammer watched their daughter climb on her father's chest. She didn't know where, or what her husband had been through in the past two days, just that he was missing and now he was back. She watched as the most important thing in their lives romped on her father, broken ankle and all.

The white Gulfstream had met the Nighthawks at Kunsan AFB and with the exception of a quick refueling stop in Hawaii, flew directly to Groom Lake in Nevada. The flight home was quiet, pensive, and somber as the remaining members of the Nighthawks thought of those who weren't making the trip back.

Chris looked out the window as Las Vegas passed beneath the plane and wondered how he was going to face Sarah, and what he would tell her. The city seemed different, changed somehow. Or maybe it's me, Chris thought as the plane made a turn towards the North and Groom Lake. The eastern sky was just starting to show the hints of morning as the Gulfstream turned on final approach to Groom Lake's runway. Chris realized that, except for nap he was able to grab in Japan, he hadn't really slept since he and the Nighthawks had left the Nevada Desert two days ago. And as much as he loved to fly, after spending twenty-eight hours in the air, all he wanted was a warm, solid, non-moving bed.

Colonel Mulgrave was at the hangar to greet the Nighthawks as they arrived, and to Chris he looked just as rough as they were.

"Gentleman welcome home. I know that even though the mission was a success, for us it was a tragic loss, and due to the extreme closeness of the team, each of you, as well as I, are feeling that loss very deeply. I'm not going to keep you here to debrief you right now, I think it's more important that you get some sleep, and a little time to deal with what has happened. If any of you want someone to talk to, my door is open.

"After you are all debriefed, the Nighthawks are officially in rest status for thirty days. I want you to use that time to be with the people that are important to you, and to take some time to deal with what you have all been through, whether that be through therapy or nature or whatever you want to do to heal. The Nighthawks will pick up the expense. Again, gentleman, good job. Now, go and get some rest; you all look like shit." Colonel Mulgrave smiled.

"You too sir," A voice from the back answered, and the rest of the Nighthawks laughed.

The Nighthawks picked up their gear and headed for the bus back to their Groom Lake rooms. Chris took this opportunity to approach Colonel Mulgrave.

"Sir, can I speak to you for a minute?"

"Sure Chris, I know how close you and Mike were. I'm sorry."

"Well sir, that's what I want to talk to you about. If you haven't broken the news to Mike's wife, Sarah, I would like to be there, when you do. I kind of made a promise to Mike, and I'd like to be able to keep it."

Colonel Mulgrave reached out and put his hand on Chris shoulder, and Chris could feel the fatigue in the man's hand.

"I think that would be a good idea, why don't you get some sleep and we'll fly back at 16:00 hours this afternoon."

"Yes sir," Chris paused, "Thank you sir."

"You're welcome. Now go get some sleep, that's an order."

"Yes sir." Chris saluted and headed for the bus back to the living quarters for some much needed rest.

Sleep didn't come easy for Chris, and the images that flashed through his mind in the disguise of short dreams, were those events of the past forty-eight hours. He could see the face of the soldier he took out by the crash site, almost mocking Chris by laughing at him right before his head exploded, and the image of Phoenix Two erupting in a yellow fireball. Chris awoke with a start to find his sheets soaked with sweat, and figured that it was futile to try to get any more sleep. Remember to see the doc about some sleeping pills, Chris thought as he entered the shower. He hoped that the water would wash away the nightmares. He knew it wouldn't. Chris knew that they were going to be a part of his life for a while, and that he could either come to terms with them, or continue to fight them and never sleep.

Both dressed in their formal uniforms, Chris and Colonel Mulgrave boarded the white Gulfstream for the flight to Las Vegas. Chris returning to the plane that had been filled with demons during the long sleepless flight home. Colonel Mulgrave watched as the thoughts crossed the young sergeant's eyes and was struck with his own demons as well. Three of his men weren't coming back — didn't come back, and now he had to face the music. It was he that had to look in the widow's eyes and tell her of her husband's death.

Colonel Mulgrave watched below as the sun reflected off of the little ponds and reservoirs on the ground and thought of the men he had just lost. Looking up he noticed that Chris hadn't moved and wished to god that he could say the right thing, find the right words to help him heal. But he knew, from his early days in Vietnam, that there was nothing that could be said to soften the loss felt when one of your own didn't return. Nothing could be said.

The plane touched down in silence and the two arrived at the front door of Sarah Hecht's house just before five o'clock. Colonel Mulgrave took a deep breath and rang the doorbell. Sarah answered the door, "Colonel, what a lovely..." and as she realized that both were wearing dress uniforms, and saw the sorrow in their eyes, it hit her. She immediately knew that every military wife's worst fear had come true. Sarah shook her head as the tears erupted from the deepest part of her soul. Chris tentatively approached Sarah and let her collapse against his chest as her tears flooded his thoughts.

After the first release had subsided, Colonel Mulgrave and Sgt. Ross escorted Sarah back inside the house and began to give her the news officially.

"As commander of his unit, it is with deepest regrets that I must inform you of the death of your husband, Staff Sergeant Michael Christopher Hecht." The Colonel paused and cleared his throat. "The helicopter on which Sergeant Hecht was a crew member experienced critical mechanical failure and crashed in the Nevada desert while conducting search and rescue training. All on board, perished."

Sarah stared out of the kitchen window as the words ricocheted off of the interior of her head like bullets in a marble room. No, God no. Anything but this, Sarah thought as her life seemed to slip out of her hands, just out of reach.

Chris gently approached Sarah and whispered. "I know it's no consolation Sarah, but he died instantly. No pain. He wasn't aware of what was happening. "

The words Sarah spoke came out stilted, at first barely audible. "How…how…why did his chopper crash?"

"Catastrophic engine failure." Colonel Mulgrave responded. "There was nothing that the pilot could do."

Chris watched as the trembling began in the tips of Sarah's fingers and slowly spread to the rest of her body. Both Chris and Colonel Mulgrave helped Sarah to the couch and Chris's heart went out to her as he wondered how he would ever be able to keep the promise that he had made to Mike. How would he ever be able to help Sarah come back to the person he knew her to be.

Colonel Mulgrave brought over a glass of water and handed it to Sarah. He knew it was a small gesture and he wanted so badly to do so much more, but he didn't know how. He barely knew who this person actually was. He knew her only as the wife of one of his men. He routinely turned down the invitations to their monthly barbecue, only attending one or two, and for that he was now sorry.

Being commander unfortunately had caused a distance between his men, their families, and himself. A distance that all of the officer manuals said was necessary, but now somehow seemed archaic and silly. These men were ready to put their lives on the line for others in need, because of an idea that had come to him in the middle of one very cold

December evening, and the rules taught him that it had to be him and them. Commander and Unit. So he was left to pick up the pieces, without any of the tools necessary. Colonel Mulgrave spoke quietly to Chris, "I need to get back to Groom Lake, I'll get your debriefing of the mission tomorrow." The Colonel then paused, "or the day after. Take as many days as she needs."

Sarah didn't even notice as Colonel Mulgrave excused himself and left her alone with Chris. She didn't notice that the Colonel and Chris both got up and went to the door. She just sat on the couch looking out the window at the Nevada sky. Colonel Mulgrave looked one last time at Sarah Hecht and saw the pain deep inside and wondered to himself if it was worth it. "Remember, I can get your debriefing once you're finished. Give her as much time as she needs."

"Yes sir." Chris answered and then closed the front door to turn his attention again towards Sarah.

She was still on the couch looking out the window, not even aware of the last moment's activities, and Chris wondered how long it would take her to heal her soul enough to notice that there was another presence in the room with her. Chris made himself comfortable, held her hand, and waited.

When Sarah had taken the time needed to incorporate into the world the unbelievable, that the person she cared most about in the world would no longer be there, she released a deep sigh and noticed for the first time since she had heard the news that there was another person in the room with her. Chris and Sarah talked, cried, and ached together most of the night, and when Chris began to leave, Sarah begged him stay the night on the couch. She didn't want to be in an empty house. It didn't matter to Chris, he knew that no matter where he slept he wouldn't get any rest anyway, and a night on a hard couch consoling a friend, was more important than sleep. And so the two friends stayed awake most of the night talking about their loss, reliving glorious memories, including the one where she had given Mike the necklace, and trying to heal what had so harshly been broken.

Chris reached his hand into his pocket and felt the thin gold chain that he had taken off of Mike in the mountains of South Korea. The thin chain was the last tangible link that he had to his best friend, but he knew in his heart where it really belonged.

"Sarah, there's something I want to give to you. I didn't think that this should be lumped in with Mike's personal effects, so I removed it as I said good bye. I think that you should keep it, it really meant a lot to him, but I think you know that."

Chris removed the chain from his pocket and placed it gently in Sarah's hand. Her eyes again swelled with tears and Chris wished to god that he could make it easier.

Sarah put her arms around her friend and barely audible, whispered. "Thank you."

Chris returned the hug and could feel the fear in Sarah's arms. The fear that if she hugged any less, she would float away. Chris knew that at this moment he was her anchor, her only proof that all of this wasn't some terrible nightmare.

The two sat quietly on the couch, neither speaking, neither moving until slowly Chris could feel the strength in Sarah's arms weaken as the fatigue gradually took over her mind and body. Chris looked out the window and could see the faint hints of dawn stretch across the morning sky as Sarah finally, out of exhaustion, placed her head on his shoulder and fell asleep.

For Sarah the new light of day also brought new promise to find out what had caused her life to change so drastically, so completely. More time to answer the questions that plagued her mind. Another chance to make sense out of the senseless. And a chance to hide from the demons that had invaded her sleep.

Chris watched as his friend's attitude changed from sorrow to pensive, and wondered what had caused the change. What demons was she now trying to battle inside her heart, and what did it have to do with him? He, of course, knew the answer and just hoped that she wouldn't put him in the position he feared most, to be loyal to friend, or to be loyal to his honor.

The question came sooner than Chris had expected it and it almost caught him off guard.

Sarah stood at the kitchen sink holding a dish towel, looking out at the flower bed that she had planted just a few days before. "Chris, how did Mike really die? What happened?"

Chris looked down at his coffee and tapped his fingers on the side of the mug.

"Sarah, it's as the Colonel said, Mike died in a helicopter crash." Well, at least that wasn't a lie, Chris thought.

The towel twisted in Sarah's hands as she continued to stare out the window. "Chris, don't you lie to me too. Tell me the truth. It wasn't an accident was it?"

"Sarah, I promise you I am not lying." Chris took a sip of the lukewarm coffee to grab a few precious moments and sort his thoughts. "It was an accident. In the worst way, it was an accident."

"But not a training accident." The way she said "training accident" was cold and a bit sarcastic, and Chris wondered what would happen if he actually did tell her.

"Look, Sarah, Mike is gone. It was an accident, something that shouldn't have happened but did. Nothing is going to change that. Just know that Mike died the man that you knew him to be. Don't do this to yourself."

Sarah turned from the sink and looked with compassion at her friend. "I'm sorry Chris, it's just that I need to know. Mike and I never lied to each other. I know he did things that he couldn't tell me about, and that's fine, but with his death, the Air Force has inserted this lie into our relationship, and it's just not fair. Why can't they just give me the dignity of telling me the truth. Who the hell would I ever tell."

Chris watched as again his friend broke down into tears and wished to God that there was something more that he could do.

20 DECISIONS

After making sure that Sarah would be all right being alone for awhile, Chris went to the canyons that he and Mike had climbed so many times together to get a perspective on what had happened. He didn't know why, but the thought of Mike's death being labeled a "training accident" bothered Chris. No, he did know why. Because a heroic death shouldn't go unnoticed. Unacknowledged.

Even though the members of the Nighthawks didn't do what they did for recognition, the families of those that died deserved to know that the people that they loved had given their lives for something much more important than a "training accident." They had given their lives in trade for someone else's.

Chris looked out over the red rocks that made up the canyon and wondered how something could be so harsh and so beautiful at the same time. It's the same as Mike's death, Chris thought. Harsh that he had died, but beautiful for the reason why. To bring a father back home to his wife and little girl. Shouldn't Sarah know the reason? That her husband sacrificed his own life so that a little girl wouldn't grow up without a father. Chris knew that Sarah didn't believe the story of a training accident; she was smarter than that. She knew that the team had been through vast amounts of training, and if it had been an exercise Mike would have called the first chance he got. Not receiving a phone call had told Sarah that something was different, something was unusual, and she had already put two and two together. It would be an insult to her intelligence to try to make her believe different.

Chris looked up at the cliff face and reached for the first handhold, for the first time feeling the fatigue in his body. Climbing had always been a sanctuary for Chris. It was part physical, mostly mental, and very meditational. By focusing on the details of the climb — handholds, footholds, etc. — the mind became clearer, sharper. Climbing had the effect of wiping away all of the flotsam and jetsam that accumulated in the human mind day in and day out.

With each finger hold that Chris reached another image of Mike would scream through his head. Images from Korea, images from previous climbs, images from barbeques. All coming in waves as Chris climbed higher and higher.

Finally reaching the top of the cliff, Chris had revisited most of the major events that had occurred in his and Mike's friendship. It had been such a short time really, but Chris knew that they would have been friends forever. And now, to honor that friendship he had to be there for Sarah. He had to make sure she survived this. He had to try and bring her out the other end, just as they had brought the Colonel out of Korea.

On top of the canyon looking out over the rocks that Mike and Chris had spent hours climbing and talking about life, Chris wondered what would happen if he broke his oath and told Sarah the truth. No one except the two of them would ever know. The question was if he could live with the knowledge that he had betrayed the rest of the team to be true to the promise that he had made to his friend. And if he did, could he live with the consequences? Could he, in his mind, handle the end of his military career for divulging something that may or may not help Sarah deal with this? It wasn't likely, but it was possible that he could be sentenced to prison for divulging classified information. The words struck him as hard as a rock thrown from his own conscience. Are you prepared to do all this? Chris looked at the shadows created by the rocks stretch like fingers across the sand. Would telling her ease any of the pain or just make it worse?

Who in truth did he owe loyalty to? If he told, no lives would be in danger, national security wouldn't be compromised, what would it harm? Yet he had always lived by the creed that his word was his bond, and if he said it he meant it. And he had given his word to the government. But he had also given it to his best friend, hadn't he? What was more important, friendship and honor or loyalty and honor?

Chris again looked to the rocks that had provided such wisdom in the past, and they remained silent. There were no answers, no clues, no help. Just silence.

Chris looked up at the sky and watched as the clouds eased to the east. Chris leaned back against the rocks and briefly closed his eyes.

When he finally awoke it was late afternoon, and the sun was starting to set behind the brick red rocks of the canyon. Chris was amazed that he had even slept at all, let alone a peaceful sleep. There were still no answers and Chris decided that the best thing he could do now would be to get on with the day to day duties of living his life. The next thing he had to do was give the Air Force his version of the mission, and that could wait until morning. Until then, he would check on Sarah and then, maybe, lose himself in the lights of the Vegas casinos.

Chris arrived back at Groom Lake to be debriefed by Colonel Mulgrave. After he was finished he could take the time off to do what he had to do for Sarah and himself and he wanted to get it over with as fast as possible. When Chris entered the Colonel's office, he was surprised to see that there was also a General, a General that Chris had never seen before, but immediately knew to be General Mitchell, in the office with Colonel Mulgrave.

"Sgt. Ross, this is General Mitchell from the Joint Chiefs of Staff, he's our muscle back at the Pentagon. Without him, we wouldn't exist."

Chris came to attention, to give the General a proper greeting, when the General smiled and stuck out his hand.

"None of that son, I just want to shake your hand. You all made us very proud over there, it was a great job you did pulling out Colonel Hammer. I understand that you're the sniper who took out the soldier with the Stinger missile."

"Yes sir, but it appears that he wasn't the one I had to worry about."

The General shook his head. "That was just a lucky shot Sergeant, if you hadn't have taken out the Stinger missile, both choppers would've been destroyed and we now would be having a funeral for fifteen men instead of six."

"I know that sir, it just hurts to be having one at all." Chris pressed his lips together in a tight smile.

Colonel Mulgrave gestured to the empty seat in front of his desk. "Well then Sergeant Ross, why don't you have a seat and tell us your account of what happened over there."

Chris moved to the chair and sat down. He had sat in this chair once before. Only then it was to get a strong reprimand for a stunt that he and the rest of his team had played on the guys at the NSA. One night, after a few hours of boredom at TOCACL, during that time when all ideas begin to seem unbelievably funny, the team decided that it would be a good idea to dye a parachute red and construct an extremely large arrow with the words "You are here" and place it in the middle of one of the test ranges for the benefit of the satellites passing overhead. Only those back at the NSA didn't think the joke was very funny and had called every person they could get a hold of at Nellis, Area 51, and Tonopah to find the creators of the prank. Although no one ever knew for sure who the perpetrators were, Colonel Mulgrave had his suspicions when one of the old parachutes had mysteriously disappeared. He had called each member of the team individually into this office and officially verbally reprimanded them. Unofficially, he had laughed and said it was one of the "best damn pranks he had ever seen", and had somehow managed to get a photo of the satellite image which now hung on the wall.

"Okay Chris, why don't you tell us what you remember."

"Well Sir, there really was nothing out of the ordinary until the crash. The mission had gone almost exactly as planned. We arrived a few miles north of the crash site and proceeded towards Colonel Hammer, encountering hostile forces as expected. They didn't know we were there until we started to take them out." The memories of the mission flooded Chris's head in bits and pieces, flashing like slides across his mind. "I took out the soldier closest to the crash site and the team moved in to get the Colonel and destroy anything left of the aircraft. A small squad of North Koreans engaged us, we returned fire until they were neutralized, and then called in the choppers." Chris paused as the memories came in slow, detached sections. "After the choppers had arrived another small squad of North Koreans approached from the lower end of the valley and engaged us with small arms fire. They may have been the same squad that had brought down Colonel Hammer because they still had a Stinger missile with them. We returned fire and I left Phoenix Two to take out the soldier with the Stinger as he was about to get a lock on us. After he was taken out, I boarded Phoenix One and we egressed the area under small arms fire from the remaining North Koreans. The next thing I remember is Phoenix Two telling Phoenix One about the shimmy they were getting just before we crossed the DMZ, and then it happened. Phoenix Two just lost all control and went in." Chris closed his eyes and took a deep breath. With all of the memories and details came the pain and emotions that Chris had tried to bottle inside since the mission.

The room remained silent for a few minutes and then Colonel Mulgrave spoke. "I think that's all we need about the mission Chris. Thank you for being so precise." Colonel Mulgrave looked towards the General. "Anything else, Sir?"

"No, I think I'm pretty much satisfied. Thank you Sergeant, you can be dismissed."

"Thank you Sir." Chris said as he rose from the chair and

came to attention.

"Oh, one more thing," Colonel Mulgrave began, "How's Sarah Hecht doing?"

Chris paused, unsure of how to answer. "She'll pull through, it will just take a while. I think that she's having a hard time believing the story of the training accident."

Colonel Mulgrave traded looks with the General before he spoke. "Well that's normal. I'm sure in time she'll come to terms with it for herself. All we can do is be there for her."

Colonel Mulgrave looked at the man in front of him. No emotion, no pain, no grief. Except for the brief moment a few moments before, he was a piece of stone. Like every well trained warrior he had pushed it down into the pit of his stomach, to be released at the funeral or at a time when it reached an explosion point and released on its own; and that's what the Colonel worried about.

"How about you? How are you doing Chris? Any plans for your convalescent leave?"

"Well I thought I might do some camping up in Utah. Just be by myself for a while, sort things out."

"Good. The leave papers have already been signed, you just have to pick them up after the General's briefing."

Chris smiled. "Thank you sir. Is there anything else?"

Colonel Mulgrave looked at the General, who shook his head and turned back to Chris. "No that will be all. You're dismissed, see you at the briefing."

Chris turned and exited the Colonel's office again feeling the uneasy confusion of what he should do about Sarah.

For the General's briefing the white Gulfstream had been moved outside to the ramp, and the remaining members of Rescue Team Alpha stood at attention in the empty hangar. An American flag hung from the rafters above their heads and the team was dressed in their formal dress uniforms as the General began to speak.

"At ease gentlemen." General Mitchell looked at the men in front of him and wondered if the medals he was about to pin on their chests were enough. "First of all let me say that the President and the rest of the Joint Chiefs of Staff are very proud of the job you did. I know that it doesn't feel like much of a victory right now, but I just want you to remember that each of you would give your life for each other, and that's all that they did. They gave their lives for Colonel Hammer's return, and I know all of you would do the same. They died doing what they wanted to do. Rescuing a downed pilot." The General paused and gestured to Colonel Mulgrave who was standing off to the side carrying 12 individual boxes.

"I know that you don't do this for the recognition, but the President and I feel that some form of thanks is in order, so by the power invested in me by the Congress of the United States you are all awarded the Meritorious Service Medal. When I call your name, please step forward to have your medal pinned to your chest.

"One of you has also been awarded the Bronze Star for bravery, and I would like to call him up first. If it had not been for this Sergeant's quick thinking and reaction, the entire mission very probably would have ended in failure, with more loss to human life. His reaction was selfless, without thought for danger or the possibility to be left behind as his chopper started to take off. I think you all know who I am talking about, and if Sergeant Christopher J. Ross would step forward, it would be my honor to pin the Bronze Star on personally."

Chris came to attention and approached the General to have both medals pinned to his chest. Chris performed the award ritual, which included shaking hands with the General, taking the award certificate with the left hand, and then popping a crisp, perfect, military salute to the General, without emotion.

The rest of the Nighthawks received their awards in the same manner each performing the perfunctory movements and saluting the General. After all of the awards had been received, the Nighthawks were briefed on the fact that the due to the nature of the mission, the awards were, of course, classified and would never be reflected in their records, unless the mission ever became declassified which was unlikely.

The awards would sit in a locker somewhere gathering dust with just the memory of the ceremony allowed to remain in the minds of the Nighthawks.

After the ceremony Chris caught the first flight back to Nellis. He wanted to check on Sarah, pack his bags, and get to Utah as soon as possible. Emotions were now starting to flood back through the wall that Chris had constructed in his mind and the pressure was beginning to get pretty intense. He could, like the little Dutch boy, keep plugging the holes, but Chris knew eventually and soon, they would come crashing out.

Chris arrived at Sarah's house just in time to see her

loading a suitcase into her car.

"Going somewhere?"

"Chris!" Sarah closed the trunk and ran to her friend, quickly giving Chris another strong hug. "I thought I'd get away for a few days, until the service. Just go somewhere and clear my head."

"Good, I think that's a good idea. I'm going to get away a little myself. Where are you going?"

"I thought I might go to Catalina Island. Mike took me there once and I know it's a place filled with good memories." Sarah glanced back at the house. "I just can't sit around this house, it's too depressing."

"Would you like some company or do you want to be alone?"

"I think, this time, it's time to be alone. I want to remember Mike in my way, cry a little, laugh a little, cry a lot." Sarah paused. "I still have some time left, would you like some iced tea?"

Chris smiled, "Always the perfect hostess huh Sarah? No thank you, I'm fine. I just stopped by to make sure you were doing okay before I go up to Utah." Chris turned more serious. "How are you doing Sarah?"

"I'm doing all right. It's tough, especially at night." Sarah stepped back, away from Chris, and leaned back on the car. "I'm dealing with it. I still have some major questions for the Air Force, but other than that I think I'll be able to handle it."

Sarah reached out and grabbed Chris's hand. "Look, Chris, I know you guys were on a classified mission. I don't know what it was, but I know Mike didn't die during a training accident, there are too many questions." Sarah brushed a tear away from her check. "I've just decided that I'm not going to deal with any of that right now. I'm going to go away, go to a place that was kind to me, remember Mike, and come back for the memorial service. After all that, I'll find out what really happened, and deal with it."

Chris looked at the women in front of him with awe. At first glance you wouldn't think she was all that strong, but after getting to know her Chris realized that she was one of the toughest people he knew.

"Well, you do what you have to do Sarah, whatever you decide I want you to know that I'll be here for you."

"I know Chris. Mike was lucky to have a friend like you, I'm lucky to have a friend like you. Now give me a hug so I can get out of here and catch my plane."

Chris hugged Sarah and walked her to the car door, helping her inside.

"I'll be back in a few days." Sarah said as she started the Honda. "In time for the memorial service."

"We'll drive over together, I'll stop by about one."

"I'd appreciate that."

Chris watched as Sarah backed out of the driveway and headed on her own quest to exorcise the demons that invaded her sleep.

After Sarah had left, Chris went back to his apartment, grabbed a few clothes to take to Utah, and headed north on I-15.

The southern mountains of Utah were only three hours from Las Vegas and Chris had discovered them on the way to his new assignment. A ski resort during the winter, during the off season the area was practically deserted and you could get a small condo for almost nothing. Chris pulled onto the small road that led to the condominium and parked the car at the far end of the parking lot.

Chris looked around at the green trees and took a deep breath. Here, at the higher altitude the air was cool and sweet and Chris wished he could spend more than the two days he had arranged.

After checking in with the front desk and dropping off his bags in the room, Chris took a walk to the local general store. The only building other than the condominium in what was considered a town. Greeted by a very friendly golden retriever, Chris picked up a few items to get through the couple of days and headed out for the top of the mountain.

Perched on the high end of the desert, the southern Utah mountains were the border between the lush and the arid. From here Chris could see the desert spread out below him like a carpet of red, stretching forever into the distance, heat rising off of the hot sand far below. Chris picked out a rock to sit on and dangled his feet over the edge of the cliff and watched.

Far below a hawk circled on the air currents, riding the thermals higher and higher until the hawk himself towered above Chris. It just follows its heart, Chris thought to himself as he watched the hawk change air currents and begin the process over again. "Life would be so much easier if I could be like you. Just following your heart and instincts, not having to worry about what's wrong or right, no promises, no commitments." Chris wondered what the hawk would say if he could hear him, if he could understand him, if he could talk back.

Chris listened and realized for the first time that there was no sound. No wind, no noise, nothing. Pure nothing, and for the first time in his life, Chris truly understood how silence could be deafening. "Talk about getting away from it all." Chris said to no one in particular as leaned back and looked at the sky. Above, the blue seemed to stretch forever, completely unbroken by clouds, only stopping at the edge of the earth to create the horizon in the distance.

"Mike, what the hell do I do now?" Chris could feel the walls that he had built during the mission start to come lose. Cracks became fissures, fissures became holes, and the emotions stored behind came crashing out. The wall was a necessity. In combat, no matter what happens, the mission must continue. The only way the human mind can operate in that kind of environment is to separate the physical from the emotional and place the emotional behind a wall of brick. But eventually that brick crumbled and then there was no choice. The emotions must be dealt with.

The tears came slowly at first, then more quickly, soon followed by the fear, confusion, and pure rage that his best friend had been taken away. Rage that Sarah had to go through the pain that she was now dealing with. And the consolation that Mike and the rest of the team had died for the most noble of reasons. To save another's life. "So that others may live."

The pain welled deep in the pit of Chris's stomach and rose through his body until the quiet of the wilderness was replaced with the painful wail of a wounded soul.

21 CLOSURE

The Nevada sky was crystal blue as the American flag blew in the light breeze. Chris looked at the manicured green lawns of the cemetery, and was hypnotized by each of the headstones as they fell in perfect geometrical lines across the freshly cut grass. So neat and clean, to hide something so dirty. Death was the ugliest thing that humans faced and yet we honored our loved ones with beauty. Chris used to find quiet and solitude in a cemetery near his home, but now, all he found was pain. The funeral was a joint service for the Nighthawks that had died during the extraction, even though the bodies other than Mike's had been sent to their families, to be buried in their hometowns, and Chris looked at the crowd that was gathered to listen to the pastor give the service. Against the deep green grass, the crisp blue uniforms and white gloves of the Air Force Honor Guard took on an almost surreal look, and Chris wondered if maybe all this wasn't some sort of highly detailed dream. A figment of his imagination, an illusion. But he knew, in his heart, that it was all too real. Chris stood next to Sarah and held her hand as he scanned the faces in the group. All of the remaining Nighthawks were there, Colonel Mulgrave, General Mitchell, and standing at the edge, Colonel Hammer. Chris imagined Colonel Hammer's daughter holding her father's hand, occasionally leaning her head against his leg and realized that, yes, it was definitely worth it. This was why he did what he did, why he was willing to put his life on the line for a stranger. He had been part of a team that had helped bring this father home to his little girl and in the process, he had been willing to trade his life for the life of that little girl, because that's who they had really rescued when they had brought home Colonel Hammer. And in his heart, he knew too, that Mike had done it for the same reasons, no matter how he died.

The service was filled with all of the traditions of a military funeral, and as the honor guard performed all the honors befitting a hero's salute, Chris stood at attention staring straight ahead, not letting the pain that he felt deep inside his soul escape.

Chris looked at the rest of the Nighthawks. Each fighting their own demons, not letting the beast get to the surface. When the guns went off for the twenty-one gun salute each had a barely perceptible flinch.

Colonel Mulgrave looked at his men and wondered how long it would take. They had been trained that emotions got in the way of the mission, and that no matter how bad it got, or how confusing things became, the mission still went on. The problem was that the emotions didn't just go away, they went away to become stronger, and at a certain point they would become stronger than any will to keep them back. It was a lesson learned in Vietnam and try as they might, no one ever came up with a way to avoid it. Post Traumatic Stress

Syndrome. They had named it. They could treat it. But there was no way to effectively avoid it. Colonel Mulgrave hoped that by giving his men all thirty days off and the blank check to do what ever they wanted, the emotions would come out sooner rather than later.

After the service most of the Nighthawks gathered together and as Chris watched Sarah place another rose on Mike's grave, he felt a hand on his shoulder and turned.

"I didn't get a chance to thank your team before you left." Colonel Hammer said as he held out his hand. "Thank you Sergeant. Thank you very much. That was some nice shooting back there."

Chris took the hand that was offered to him and shook it. "You're very welcome, sir."

"You do realize that your team no longer has to buy their drinks at TOCACL or the Goatsucker. I've taken care of them for a very long time. Me and the rest of the pilots up range."

"Thank you sir, I'll have to remember that."

Chris looked back at the grave and noticed that Sarah was walking towards Colonel Mulgrave. Uh Oh. I don't think this is going to be pretty. Chris thought as he watched her approach.

"Could you excuse me for a moment sir? I think I have to run some interference for a friend."

"Of course Sergeant. See you at the laundry."

Sarah Hecht waited until he was alone before approaching Colonel Mulgrave with her questions. So many things that need to be answered, she thought as she moved through the crowd of military personnel that were between her and the Colonel, and now's the time to start.

"Colonel, can I have a word with you?"

Colonel Mulgrave turned towards the voice that had appeared out of nowhere. "Of course Sarah, what's on your mind?"

"I need to know some things about my husband's death Colonel."

This one's going to be tough Colonel Mulgrave thought as he began his answer. "What do you need to know Sarah? I've told you everything there is."

"I need to know how he really died, I know it wasn't a training accident. I want the truth. What was Mike doing when he died? Why is it a secret? Why are you keeping the truth from me?"

Seeing the pain in Sarah's face, Colonel Mulgrave wanted more than anything else in the world at that moment, to be able to tell her the truth. To ease her pain, and tell her, yes, her husband was a hero. That he didn't die in vain. But he knew he couldn't.

"It was a training accident Sarah, I'm sorry but there's nothing else to tell you. There are no secrets."

The anger in Sarah's eyes flamed, "I deserve the truth Colonel. That man was my husband. I need a chance to heal. I need to know what really happened, where it really happened, I need closure." Sarah turned to walk away but stopped. "Damn you. Damn you and your secrets. I don't care about your little secrets. About your secret fucking base. About your secret fucking missions. But don't you stand there and insult my intelligence by telling me that there aren't any. I deserve to know how my husband died, what was worth his life and the lives of the others. And one way or another I'm going to find out the truth. From you or from the Pentagon." Sarah pushed passed Colonel Mulgrave and stormed off across the manicured lawns of the cemetery.

Colonel Mulgrave let out a deep sigh and wondered just how much national security would be damaged by telling the families the truth as he watched Sarah Hecht walk into the distance to control her rage. As he contemplated the right or wrong of what he had just done, he noticed Chris follow Sarah to the side of the pond, and at that moment Colonel Mulgrave would lay odds that Chris was about to break an oath.

He had known for the last few days that Chris had been wrestling the same demons that he himself had faced years earlier in Laos. He too had been part of a classified mission during the end of the Vietnam War, and watched as a good friend had given his life for that of another. He had wanted so badly to tell how his friend really died, justify his death in the eyes of his family, but he didn't. He, at the time, had told himself that he didn't break the oath out of duty. Out of discipline. But in reality he knew that he didn't tell because he didn't know what consequences telling the truth would cause, and he didn't want to be in the eye of that kind of storm.

Over the past few days he had watched Chris battle with his conscience. He knew that Chris's friendship with Mike and through him with Sarah was stronger than any sense of duty, any sense of secrecy, or any sense of loyalty that he felt, especially since the mission was now over and no lives would be at risk. It was all in his psyche profile. Chris Ross valued friendship and family above all else, including his own life. Colonel Mulgrave knew that Chris would tell, the question was, did it really matter?

Chris watched as his friend toiled with the anger that was

raging inside her head, and walked up beside her as she stood by the pond. All she wants is to be told the truth. Chris watched the ducks swim on the water. She just wants to end this part of her life without any questions. Chris reached out and took her hand in his as he looked her in the eyes, and with one sentence, nine individual words, Chris Ross, Sergeant, twenty-four years old, put the rest of his career in jeopardy.

"Sarah, what I'm about to tell you is classified..."

ABOUT THE AUTHOR

John Harbour is a former member of the US Air Force. He lives in
New York with his wife.

Website: www.johnharbour.com

.

www.ingramcontent.com/pod-product-compliance
Lightning Source LLC
Chambersburg PA
CBHW060323260626
47160CB00007B/2663